Fooling In Love

S J Crabb

Copyrighted Material

Copyright © S J Crabb 2019

S J Crabb has asserted her rights under the Copyright, Designs and Patents Act 1988 to be identified as the Author of this work.

This book is a work of fiction and except in the case of historical fact, any resemblance to actual persons, living or dead, is purely coincidental.

All rights reserved. No part of this book may be reproduced or transmitted in any form without written permission of the author, except by a reviewer who may quote brief passages for review purposes only.

NB: This book uses UK spelling.

Contents

More books by S J Crabb

Prologue

Chapter One

Chapter Two

Chapter Three

Chapter Four

Chapter Five

Chapter Six

Chapter Seven

Chapter Eight

Chapter Nine

Chapter Ten

Chapter Eleven

Chapter Twelve

Chapter Thirteen

Chapter Fourteen

Chapter Fifteen

Chapter Sixteen

Chapter Seventeen

Chapter Eighteen
Chapter Nineteen
Chapter Twenty
Chapter Twenty-One
Chapter Twenty-Two
Chapter Twenty-Three
Chapter Twenty-Four
Chapter Twenty-Five
Chapter Twenty-Six
Chapter Twenty-Seven
Chapter Twenty-Eight
Chapter Twenty-Nine
Chapter Thirty
Chapter Thirty-One
Chapter Thirty-Two
Chapter Thirty-three
Epilogue
Note from the Author
More Books

More books by S J Crabb

The Diary of Madison Brown
My Perfect Life at Cornish Cottage
My Christmas Boyfriend
Jetsetters
More from Life
A Special Kind of Advent
Fooling in love
Will You

sjcrabb.com

♥

Prologue

Now is probably not the best time to admit I hate going to the hairdressers. I'm sitting in the dreaded chair shrouded in one of those strange black capes that remind me of Batman, completely at another's mercy.

All around me is the chatter of women making polite conversation and pretending to enjoy the experience. They must be pretending because quite frankly I would rather go to the dentists and have a root canal. At least *they* don't pretend that it's fun. You know it's going to hurt like crazy but is a necessary evil. Hairdressers smile as they drag the harsh metal comb through your tangled tresses. They grin as the tears pool in your eyes while they tear your hair out by the roots. Then they shower you with scalding water as you lean back on some sort of neck torture device while they dig their nails into your scalp all in the name of beauty.

No, I hate going to the hairdressers, which is why I'm curious as to why I'm even here in the first place?

Then I remember and the guilt hits me.

I shouldn't be.

I should be streets away in a meeting that's been arranged for months. I even had one of those notifications on my phone reminding me. Guiltily, I picture my phone in my bag, silenced and hidden away much like I am now.

The heat spreads through my body making me feel as if I'm experiencing early menopause. That would be Karma. Payback for letting everyone down just to hide out here in Hell.

My torturer/hairdresser slams a mug of tea on the shelf in front of me along with a pile of trash magazines.

"Here you go, lovely. You can cook for a while until the colour takes hold. I'll just see to my blow and go."

She winks suggestively and I stifle a smile as I reach for a magazine I usually disregard. However, today is different. Today normal has been replaced by impetuous abandon and today I'm out of my comfort zone and playing truant. All of my responsibilities have been left firmly outside because today I've had enough.

For years I've worked longer than most people and put everything into it. I have a nice flat, car and all the trappings of a working woman. I even have a man who wants to marry me and that's where the problem lies. There's a part of me that's unsure. What if he's not the one? You know, the man in the movies who brings the heroine to her knees. Her soulmate who makes her world complete. Is that Spencer? I'm not so sure anymore.

We work together, eat together, sleep together and rarely play together and this was the next logical step. My life runs like a machine and nothing is left to chance. My day is planned out months in advance and any deviations must be agreed in writing and emailed to the relevant people to keep them informed.

Yes, if they knew where I was now all hell would break loose. As I take a sip of my tea, I open the magazine. Time to switch off and become normal for however long it takes my hair to cooperate. I should make the most of this because as sure as the extra sugar in my tea, it won't happen again.

The seat next to me is taken by a young, glamorous, blonde. She smiles at her reflection in the mirror as the hairdresser looks at her with approval. Yes, she's obviously one of them. Those women who head here religiously every week. This is the mother ship and shamelessly I listen in on their conversation.

"So, honey. What will it be today, the usual?"

The woman speaks in a soft, girly, voice – actually, she lisps adorably.

"Oh, please, Donna. Make me look beautiful because today is going to be amazing."

Donna smiles indulgently and softly strokes the woman's hair lovingly. None of the pain inflicted on the masses for this woman. She is revered and loved as the obviously important customer she is.

Almost sighing, Donna runs her fingers through the hair of the woman who looks as if she's just stepped out of the magazine I'm holding. They make eye contact and the girl smiles smugly and whispers just loud enough for the whole world to hear.

"I think he's going to propose today."

Donna shrieks which makes me almost spill my tea. Frantically, I try to stop the liquid splashing on to Batcape and start to think I may hate this woman sitting next to me.

She giggles. "Yes, I'm heading off to meet him now. We're having lunch which is unusual in itself."

Donna raises a quizzical eyebrow which quite fascinates me as they appear to be drawn on with a sharpie.

"Ooh, tell me more."

Perfect woman sighs wistfully.

"Well, he's a real catch, Donna. I met him on Tinder last month and quite honestly my ship came in that day. He is everything. Good looking, well spoken, manners of a prince and the body of a sportsman."

Donna looks a little green as she continues.

"Well, he is also rich because I've never had anyone treat me so well. Jewellery, clothes, five-star nights away and flowers almost daily."

She giggles. "He likes to spoil me and who am I to argue with that? Anyway, we've spoken about getting away from it all overseas but he's so important and busy he doesn't have time for it. He told me he needed to settle down with a wife who will distract him from business. He wants one woman to take care of the machine – his words but quite appropriate if you know what I mean."

They both giggle and I almost join in. Suddenly, I can see the appeal of this place. This is so much fun, listening to the idle chatter of women with nothing better to do. Maybe there's something in this after all.

She carries on. "Well, as I said before, he's so busy and works really hard. So, last night he called and asked me to meet him for lunch at Saracen's. You know, the posh place on Bond Street. Well, you don't just grab a sandwich in there, Donna. That place is special and if the roses I received this morning are anything to go by, I think this is it. The day he cements our future and asks me to marry him."

Donna looks unsure.

"Are you sure, Camilla? I mean, it's only been a month. Maybe it's something else."

Hmm, she looks like a Camilla. I should have known. Why wasn't I called Camilla? It sounds so posh and popular. Rachel doesn't quite have the same ring to it. I need to be an 'A' name. Arabella, Camilla, Araminta, Cinderella… they scream success and I feel cheated.

They carry on and I lean a little closer to hear over the noise of the dryer.

"Well, I grabbed a new outfit in Chloe and when my hair is styled amazingly, the scene will be set. He won't want to let me go and as sure as the Jimmy Choo's I'm wearing aren't fake, I'm going to have a Tiffany diamond on this finger by the end of the day."

She holds up her finger and we all admire the polished perfection of her manicured digit. Yes, a ring would look good on there. I'm excited for her.

Then Donna says innocently, "So, who is this man made in heaven?"

Camilla giggles and stares dreamily into the magic mirror.

"Spencer Scott. He runs Viking foods, you know, the company responsible for that new Vegan ready meal range that everyone's talking about."

Donna nods, looking impressed, while I watch my world shatter and fall into the cut hair at my feet. The Tiffany diamond on my finger flashes angrily as it yells, "What the hell just happened? Spencer frigging Scott is your fiancé! Wrestle the bitch to the ground and tear her hair out by the roots. Fight for your man and tell her he's taken."

Instead, I sit on that angry diamond and retreat into my shell. I hear no more conversation, just the sound of my own life shifting. Something just happened that changes everything and I have exactly one hour to figure out what I'm going to do about it?

One hour later and I'm a new woman in every sense of the word. I stride from that hairdresser tossing my new blonde locks behind me. My ring sparkles in the sunlight and reminds me of urgent business. Yes, I need to get to Bond Street and fast.

Hailing a taxi, I make the journey that will tell me what I need to know. The driver whisks me there like an approaching army ready to do battle. I actually feel great. I love my new look and walk with confidence. I'm wearing a sharp suit that makes me feel strong and powerful and I try to ignore the part of me that's actually hoping this is all true.

For the last hour, every possible scenario played out in my mind. Camilla was talking of that other Spencer Scott who runs Viking foods in a parallel universe. Sliding doors in real life – my life and this will all have been an amazing mistake.

However, I know it's true. Of course, it is. Spencer's a player and always has been. I've pushed aside the rumours of the office dalliances. Scoffed at the women who turn up at reception demanding his time. Gritted my teeth at the envious looks of women who openly flirt with him and discounted any tales of sightings in seedy bars at night. No, Spencer and I are a formidable team and work well together. Of course, he loves me because he tells me every night in bed before switching off the light. I'm the one who receives the perfunctory roses on Valentine's day sent to the office designed to impress. I'm the one who has been told to clear my diary to plan our wedding and I'm the one who fields the calls of the estate agents searching for our dream forever home. Not Camilla, perfect hair and nails, Jimmy Choo wearing Barbie doll. Me, Rachel Asquith, all round super person and the love of his life.

By the time we reach Bond Street I'm ready to do battle. Yes, I will find out once and for all and confront them. If it is him, I'd like to see him talk his way out of this one.

As I stride towards the impressive doors of Saracen's, my step falters. I start to slow down as something changes. What if it is him – what then? Maybe he wants to end it with me but doesn't know how? Will I be the one who leaves with nothing? However, there's one voice inside my head that won't go away.

'What if you disappear? Start again and leave this all behind. Go far away and forget all about Viking foods and cheating fiancés.'

I must look like a crazy person because quite frankly I'm walking in slow motion like a robotic dancer. I see the looks all around me, raised eyebrows and shaking heads. 'Madwoman alert, call the crazy police.'

So, with a sigh, I step to the side and away from the restaurant doors. I move to the side of the building and shadow the window instead. Maybe, I'll just take a look inside. It's silly to make a scene if there's not one to see.

Removing my sunglasses from my bag, I cover my eyes. I am now officially in disguise because my hair has changed colour from light brown to platinum blonde and I'm wearing a bright red lipstick for once.

Carefully, like a private investigator, I glance in as though I'm looking for someone. Well, I am and my heart jumps as I see him. Yes, there's no mistaking it, Spencer Scott, aka cheating asshole, sits there gazing into the eyes of Camilla flaming bimbo. They are holding hands across the table and I watch as he smoulders across from her. Who does the idiot think he is smouldering away like that in public? She is openly flirting with him and bats her fake eyelashes making me hope they fall into his food.

Yes, there's no mistaking it, Spencer is cheating on me during the day when I'm supposed to be several miles from here, tied up in a meeting that sucks the will to live out of you. Here he is, secure in the knowledge that nobody will see them because nobody else can frigging well afford to eat their lunch in this billionaire's playground. What the hell is he playing at?

Turning around, I fight to breathe. Any tears that show themselves are blinked away angrily. How dare he? In fact, how dare he a million times, because I'm no fool. I know in my heart Camilla is just one of many and there will be more in the future. I'm under no illusions and am tired of it all.

Moving away, I start walking. The only companion I take with me is change. The office is in the other direction but my minds made up.

I'm getting as far away from here as possible. They can cope without me because for the first time in my life – I'm walking away.

"I hope you'll be really happy here."

Looking around me, I'm sure I will. The pretty cottage by the sea is just what the doctor ordered. Perivale is one of those sparkling stars in the universe that fell to earth and took root. This place is perfect and even the sun is shining as it catches the light of the sea and makes everything sparkle.

The agent smiles at me happily. "You know, Rachel. You're so lucky this was available. Thank goodness that old Mrs Steeplehead needed hospitalisation and the subsequent care home. You were lucky there."

Shaking my head, I don't think Mrs Steeplehead would see things quite the same way. I feel like an intruder as I look around at her worldly possessions that are steeped in history and held together with memories. I feel a pang as I think about the poor woman who called this place home. Apparently, she suffered a fall while changing the light bulb and broke her hip. Her family waded in and arranged for her to move into the care home for her own protection. They decided to rent out her home, fully furnished, to help with the bills. I feel sorry for her because what she's left behind is a little gem.

Verity, the agent, throws open the window and the fresh, salty, air, invades the room. "Take a deep breath, Rachel. This place has healing powers."

I mumble to myself. "Tell that to Mrs Steeplehead."

She carries on rambling.

"There's a coastal path that takes you to Pembury, the nearest town. It's about an hour's walk but can be quite invigorating. The nearest house is two minutes' walk away and you'll love Bert and Sheila Richardson. Across the road is Sally Mumble. She lives on her own with her cat and you'll probably see her whizzing around on her Pashley."

I raise my eyes and she laughs. "Bike. You know the sort, the one with a basket on the front. Occasionally you'll see the cat in the basket. Sally's a little eccentric but nice enough."

She points to a building on the hill in the distance.

"That's the big house. It's empty for most of the year but word is, the owner's heading home soon. He's a pilot and doesn't hang around much. I heard he's bringing his family to stay for the summer."

I follow her around the little cottage and feel calm for once. This place is magical and nothing at all like what I'm used to.

London seems another planet in comparison. I've heard about places like this. They are behind the times and steeped in tradition. No mod cons and living life as they used to before the world went mad and greed took over. However, the best thing of all is that nobody will think of looking for me here. This place is perfect in every way.

Verity claps her hand and says loudly, "Right then, I'll leave you to settle in and get acquainted with the place. If you need anything, call me. Just don't pull those cords that dangle everywhere, otherwise, you'll have the ambulance turn up. I did tell them to remove them but nobody ever listens to me. You mark my words; something will happen and I can say 'I told you so.' Anyway, Rachel, enjoy your new home, and I hope you'll be very happy here."

I see her out and as the door closes behind her, I relax. Finally, I can breathe again and put the city behind me and all the stress with it.

All I have is packed in my hire car. A few cases of clothes and possessions but nothing to remind me of the life I've left.

Happily, I explore the little cottage that I fell in love with as soon as I saw the picture. Bluebell cottage is a stereotype of the nicest kind. A little wooden house painted blue with roses trailing around the porch. Wooden floors with threadbare rugs hold in place the many antiques that must have many stories to tell. Cotton curtains made by hand, billow at the windows as the sunlight shines on every shadow chasing it away. The cottage is basic but clean and I'm happy with my choice.

There's a little wood burner in the fireplace and a chintz-covered settee set before it.

The kitchen is basic and made out of painted white wood. A small pine table and four chairs stand by the window overlooking the shimmering sea. All I can hear are the sounds of seagulls overhead and the gentle lap of the waves on the beach below.

I decide to hold off unpacking and make the most of this glorious day. Heading outside, I notice the Spring flowers have passed their best and wilt in the sunshine. As I set off to explore, I feel as free as the birds who circle above looking for food. Who needs a man? I don't. I am now officially single and not willing to mingle. Not that I expect to find anyone here worth mingling with. No, the priority now is me and I'm going to make sure that *me* is happy before anything.

The tiny garden is a little wild but I can see the remnants of what it once was. Broken, faded trellis is held up by rambling roses. The grass is poking through the cracks in the paving stones and weeds flourish where flowers once shone, surrounded by discarded broken pots and a watering can without its rose.

A metal bench sits rusting under a tree and a stone birdbath now just holds weeds.

Moving through the little broken gate at the end I find myself walking towards the coastal path. The urge to reach the beach is strong, so I walk with enthusiasm to the steps cut into the side of the cliff that will take me there.

As I make the climb, I push any worries away. What I have just done is impulsive, destructive and selfish and I couldn't care less. I left London and Viking foods behind without even so much as a goodbye. All I left was a message that I was taking a break and would let them know when I'd be back. It's not as if I'm not owed time off. I've never taken any, except for the odd day here and there for weddings, funerals and long weekends away. Just for a moment, I picture Spencer's face when he finds out. I almost wish I was there to see the anger and irritation on his face at not knowing what's going on. He'll find out I was never at that stupid meeting that he arranged and won't know about my meeting with his latest conquest.

I'm sure he'll try to find me, after all, we do live together. However, I've left no trail and taken nothing but my purse and a few clothes. I'm pretty sure I'm safe from him turning up and demanding my return.

As soon as I reach the beach, I'm happy I came. I can't remember the last time I went to the beach. Certainly, not in this country and I wonder why I've left it so long. As I look around, it strikes me this place is like a postcard. A beautiful bay with a sandy beach and the cool crystal waters sparkle before me, welcoming me to test them out.

There's a tiny breeze that calms the waves and the sun is shining brightly in the sky. As I look around, I see nothing but nature and feel happy inside. Quickly, I remove my shoes and allow my toes to curl in the sand. It feels so soft and tickly and I giggle like a school girl inside.

Sitting down, I run my fingers through the sand and relish the softness of the silky grains that sift through them. Just a simple pleasure that costs nothing but time. My time has always been valuable but I am fast realising you can't put a price on this feeling. Freedom.

For a while, I lie back and let the sun warm my soul and notice the difference around me. Sounds are clearer, the different smells weave a tapestry of life here and the temperature warms the chill in my heart.

Soon the sun intensifies, and the sea beckons. A quick look around shows me I'm alone so before I can change my mind, I remove my dress and leave it abandoned with my reservations on the sand.

The sea welcomes me in like an old friend. The icy waters invigorate rather than chill and I swim happily for a while, just floating on my back without a care in the world. As I lie floating in paradise, I feel as if I can conquer the world. I am now officially a free spirit and will catch my own food and exist off the land. I will learn about nature and make my own medicines and the clothes I'll wear will be made by hand. I'll learn to live again and nobody can ever tell me what to do ever again.

"Oi, you can't swim there. Didn't you see the signs?"

Suddenly, I'm brought back from my Nirvana to reality and quickly look up.

A man is watching me from a speedboat that quite frankly must be the Tesla of the sea because I never heard it coming. He shakes his head and says in a much slower voice. "I… said… you… can't… swim… here… get… out."

What! How dare he speak to me as if I'm an idiot?

I throw him my most disdainful look and say haughtily, "There are no signs and why may I ask, can't I swim here? Do you own it or something?"

He rolls his eyes and stares at me with the look usually reserved for the crazies.

"Jellyfish."

Oh my god, what?! I look around frantically as I search the water for the evil little suckers. He starts to laugh as I flounder around in panic, which only adds to my mood. I say angrily, "Stop laughing and give me a hand, will you?"

He grins wickedly. "If you throw in a please, I'll consider it."

I shriek as my hand brushes against something soft and slimy and then before I know what's happening, two strong capable man hands grab me under the arms and haul me into the boat. The water pours off me like Niagara Falls as I fall to a heap on the floor. "Ouch."

He looks concerned. "What's the matter, have you been stung?"

I gaze up at him irritably. "I don't think so but you threw me in like a sack of coal and I hit my foot on some sort of metal object. Thanks for that by the way, I think I'd have been safer with the Jellyfish."

He shakes his head and sits on the driving seat and studies me like a prize fish he caught. Suddenly, I'm aware that all I have between me and mother nature is my underwear that appears to be the transparent kind when wet. Looking down, I scream with mortification and try to use my own body to cover my embarrassment as he rakes me in from head to toe. I scream at him angrily, "Pervert. Is this how you get your kicks? Preying on young women with fanciful tales of Jellyfish dangers to get them in your boat. Don't you have an oilskin or something?"

He laughs out loud. "Oilskin? You're hilarious. Here, cover up with this. I don't want it back, it's not my colour, anyway."

Furiously, I grab the fleece he's holding out and pull it over my head. It completely covers me and drags to my knees and he laughs again. Then for the first time, I look at him. I mean - *really* look at him. This man is like a feral Ross Poldark. His hair is long and wild and his eyes as dark as Heathcliff's. His t-shirt is obviously too small for him and torn in all the right places. He's wearing cut-offs which leads the eye down to a very crowded area with muscle riddled legs that would make a lady shave cower in fear.

He looks to be around his late thirties because this is no boy. Standing before me is one hundred percent Alpha male and for once in my life I'm speechless.

He continues to look at me, actually he stares at me and I feel as if he has stripped me naked and hung me out for his pleasure. I feel extremely self-conscious and look around, then down and then up to the sky. In fact, anywhere but him.

Trying to evade his eyes I cough nervously. "Um… anyway… thanks and everything but I should be getting back."

He says with amusement. "And how do you think you'll manage that? The only thing between you and the beach is a sea full of Jellyfish. I'm in as far as I can go without the engine hitting the bottom, so what do you suggest?"

I look to the shore and see it fast disappearing. My clothes lay where I left them and I can see he's right. There's no way back.

He continues to watch me with *that look* and I try to remember that I'm good at solving problems so say in my most no-nonsense voice, "Ok, you can take me to the nearest shore and I'll call a cab. There, problem solved."

He rolls his eyes and smirks, which immediately gets my back up. "Where do you think you are, darling, London? The only cab around here is the one on my truck."

My mouth opens but nothing comes out and he looks at me as if I'm an idiot and sighs heavily. "Listen, I'll take you home. I'm just about done for the day, anyway."

Feeling somewhat relieved I say thankfully, "That's very kind of you. I hope it's not putting you out."

Once again, he takes a long lingering look and his eyes strip me bare. Then his eyes flash and he smirks, "Think nothing of it. I'm going that way and you can pay me in kind."

I almost fall into the sea as I stutter, "What the hell are you talking about? I'm paying no one in… um… kind. What's the matter with you, haven't you heard that it's the 21st century and women actually have choices? Haven't you heard about money and failing that Apple pay? Good god, what sort of man are you preying on innocent women and demanding sexual favours? I should report you to the police."

He starts to laugh which takes me by surprise and I glare at him and snarl. "What's so funny – pervert?"

He turns around and starts the engine which throws me a little and I fall against him. With one hand, he reaches out and tucks me behind him on the boat and the wind carries his words across. "What I meant was you can repay me by doing me a favour. I need a date to a fancy function and you'll do nicely."

I have no choice but to cling on as the boat gathers speed. As I bury my face in his back, I can't believe what's happening. A date! With him! He has got to be kidding. However, as my face remains pressed against him and I smell the muskiness coming from him like pheromones, I reason with myself. After all, it's only a business deal, a favour for a favour. Where's the harm in that?

♥2

By the time we reach land, I've reasoned with every argument my head has thrown at me.

What's the harm here?

Yes, he's a stranger - I know he could be a murderer.

For goodness' sake he's hot, I mean, really hot; the stuff in those books I've read on my kindle during my natural breaks.

Ok, he's rough - I might like a bit of rough.

I know he's a man and I'm sworn off them for good, but he's a MAN - all man and I owe it to my lady parts to indulge the dream a little.

Spencer would hate him – good, that's the biggest plus point.

He could be married - I doubt that he's so rude.

Ok then, he may steal your heart and then where would you be?

Back where I started, so you see 'head', I'm going whether you like it or not.

He moors the boat at a wooden jetty and grins. "Here we are. After you."

His eyes flash and I realise I have to haul myself out of here with him watching and judging me. Drawing myself up, I take a deep breath. Yes, I've got this. Get out of this boat - no problem.

Reaching up, I grip the wooden jetty and just hang there for a bit. Mm, it is rather high but I've done gymnastics in my youth. Not quite the trapeze but I'm sure I can pull myself up. So, with a little jump, I press down on the jetty and try to hook one of my legs up. Panting slightly, I fix my determination in place and use every ounce of strength I own to pull my body up. With one leg dangling and one on the jetty, I swing the other to meet it.

As I lie face down on the floor, I feel the boards sag a little as he jumps from the boat. Looking down, I can see he used a drop-down ladder from the side and hear him say with amusement. "Impressive. Do you always do things the hard way?"

I feel my face flame with embarrassment and try to act as normally as possible. "Yes, actually. I mean, where's the fun in doing things the easy way. I mean, life's a challenge, or at least I like to think so. You can take the easy road but not me. Oh no, I like a challenge. Always have done always will. In fact, I'm quite disappointed in you."

He grins. "And why is that?"

I shrug. "I don't know, I had you down as an adventurer. You know, the sort that lives life to the full. An action man that likes a challenge. Quite frankly, not the sort who resorts to steps to aid his exit. Next, you'll be telling me you have a gardener and a man to wash your car. You're probably an accountant that sits at his desk all day shuffling numbers. Not me though, I like danger and excitement. Yes, that's me, a free spirit. Anyway, I should be going. Is your truck far?"

I look around hopefully and then feel him behind me. He is so close I can hear his breathing and I'm ashamed to admit in my mind he takes me now, right here on this jetty in full view of anyone with a set of binoculars.

He leans down and whispers, "Who said we were taking the truck?"

He moves past me and my eyes follow him to what can only be described as a beast waiting to pounce. Orange flames decorate the side of the biggest, dirtiest, motorbike I have ever seen.

He throws me a jacket with 'Harley Davidson' emblazoned on the back, quickly followed by a helmet. Then he sits astride the beast and brings it to life under his thighs. Feeling disturbed that I'm jealous of a bike all of a sudden, I say angrily, "No! Absolutely one hundred percent, cotton picking, not in hells chance. Bring the truck around immediately."

He looks across and raises his eyes. "Come on, you live for adventure – remember?"

Realising I'm firmly buried up to the neck in the hole I've dug, I look down at my bare legs and cling on to the last bit of hope I have left.

"Sorry, I expect there are laws against riding barelegged. I'm sure it will contravene every traffic violation written since they were invented. I mean, I'm disappointed and everything but what can I say, rules are rules."

Quickly, I look around for a policeman or at least a traffic warden but with a sinking feeling, I can see we are the only ones here.

He shrugs. "Your choice. You either walk or tuck yourself behind me and I'll have you home in no time."

Once again, my own body betrays me and my legs can't get me there quickly enough. My arms reach for him like a demanding child and my face longs to inhale that heady scent of man. This helmet is an inconvenience because it prevents me from doing just that. However, when he runs his hands down my bare legs and pulls them tightly to his, I almost pass out. So much for new beginnings. I've forgotten and packed the idiot inside me and brought her along. When will I ever learn?

Despite the man in front of me, I think I'm having the best day of my life.

Speedboats - check.

Hot man and I'm talking *real* man – check.

Motorbike – check.

Hot date - check.

The trouble is, this man's personality appears to rub me up the wrong way. I spend so much time trying to be clever, I look anything but. I know he can see through me and that angers me more than anything. So, as we draw up outside Bluebell cottage, I try to hold on to the last shred of dignity I have left and hold out my hand. "Thank you… um… I didn't quite catch your name."

He takes my hand and says shortly, "Logan."

I smile politely. "Rachel."

Looking down at the fleece I'm wearing, I say airily, "I'll make sure to wash this and return it as soon as possible, Thanks for your help but I should be heading inside to clean up."

He nods and then says abruptly. "7.30. Dress to impress."

Before I can even reply, he kicks the bike into life and then he's gone, leaving me staring after him not knowing what on earth just happened.

♥3

I wish I could say the shower made me feel better but I think shower is the wrong word to use when describing what passes for one in Bluebell cottage. A few trickles of mainly lukewarm water make it difficult to get any part of me wet, let alone wash my hair. How on earth am I meant to clean myself here? The bath looks as if it's seen better days and has a rust patch near the plug and god only knows what caused the stain around the rim. Sighing, I try to at least run a bath but I could go out with my date and it would still be running when I came home. This is a disaster.

I resort to filling the washing-up bowl and having a strip wash. You know, like they did in the MIDDLE AGES!

Maybe this wasn't the best idea I've ever had. This isn't me. I'm used to every mod con going, and it seemed like a romantic notion at the time. The trouble is, the reality is not living up to the dream and I'm fast reconsidering my options.

Once I feel almost like my old self, I decide to go and say 'hi' to my new neighbours. Maybe they can recommend a place that has showering facilities nearby. I don't know, maybe a sports club or gym, perhaps?

First stop is Sally Mumble. I'm curious to meet her. Maybe we will share things in common and become firm friends. I could certainly use one right now so I paste the brightest smile on my face and knock on her rather tatty door.

It takes a while and I hear her moving around inside for quite some time before she opens the door.

When she does make an appearance, I see a woman around thirty or maybe forty, dressed in a kaftan with her hair dyed blue. She's wearing glasses and holds a paintbrush that's dripping a weird shade of orange onto her clothes.

She says loudly, "I saw you moving in earlier. I would have come and said 'hi' but had this job on so thought I'd call over later. I'm Sally, by the way, come in and I'll dig out some cake, I'm sure to have some around here."

I follow her in and pick my way through various pots and piles of random objects on the floor. Like the woman, her house is mismatched and messy. I'm pretty sure they could film one of those clean-up programmes in here because I can't see the floor for dust and mess.

However, Sally is lovely. She looks at me and smiles warmly and puts the paintbrush in a nearby plant pot, dabbing a little paint on the green leaves as she does. "Welcome to Perivale. Rachel, isn't it?"

Nodding, I hold out the little posy of wildflowers I picked from the garden.

"Yes, and I was told your name's Sally."

She nods and takes the flowers happily. "Wow, my favourites. I just love daisies; how did you know?"

Shaking my head, I smile. "Lucky guess. I hope you don't mind me dropping in on you, you look as if you're busy."

She shakes her head. "Not really. I said I'd paint a banner for the village hall. They're looking for volunteers to help with a fundraiser."

I say with interest. "What for?"

"The usual. The place is falling down and they need to tart it up a bit. Trouble is, it would take a lottery grant to make that place habitable. A few cake sales and Jumble sales aren't going to make a dent in that particular benevolent fund."

Feeling curious, I ask, "How much do they need?"

She shrugs. "Who knows? It doesn't matter though, not many people use it so it won't matter. This place is hardly busy at the best of times which is why I like it here."

I have to agree with her. "Yes, it does have a certain appeal. So, tell me what I can expect living here."

Sally rummages around in her cupboard and says triumphantly, "There you are."

She places a strange looking cake on the only piece of the kitchen counter that's clear and proceeds to cut a large piece for both of us.

"Well, it's quiet which is good, so that's a plus. There's not much to do, so that's another plus. Nobody ever comes here which is great. The beach is amazing but full of jellyfish so that's a problem, really. Oh, and the seagulls mess all over your washing so it's best to look out for that."

I feel faint. "So, um… Sally, what do you do with your time?"

She crams a large piece of cake in her mouth and mumbles, "Nothing."

Sighing, I tentatively take a bite of the cake, fully expecting it to be well past its sell-by date. However, I'm pleasantly surprised, as what hits my taste buds is a little piece of heaven. Just for a minute, I don't speak. Like Sally, I cram as much as the cake as possible into my mouth and revel in the taste sensation it creates.

I'm almost tempted to lick the crumbs from both our plates that are suspiciously painted orange and say with amazement, "Sally, did you make this?"

She nods. "Yeah, I can't remember what it is though. I think I used violets from the garden in the icing."

Laughing, I say, "Well, whatever it is, it's the best I've ever tasted. When you can remember will you write down the recipe for me? I'd love to try to bake it myself."

Sally smiles and I notice the years fall away. Maybe she's younger than I thought and I stare at her with fascination. Then her eyes light up as a little furry bundle of joy leaps onto the table and purrs adorably. "Meet Vixen. She's my fur baby and the only friend I can count on."

Reaching out, I stroke the sweet little cat and say softly, "She's perfect. How old is she?"

Sally looks thoughtful. "I think she's three but then again, she could be four. You know, time has no meaning here, I sometimes forget to track it."

I decide that Sally is the oddest, strangest, weirdest person I have ever met, yet strangely the most fascinating. She is so different from the usual people I mix with and yet I'm guessing her life is much more interesting.

Vixen jumps down and heads outside and Sally looks at me with interest. "Have you met anyone yet?"

I shiver as I think of Logan and try to make my voice sound as normal as possible as I say lightly, "Oh yes, somebody called Logan."

Sally's eyes widen. "What, Logan Rivers?"

Typical. Trust him to have some kind of rock star name. I look interested. "Do you know him?"

She shakes her head. "No."

Feeling as if I'm in a parallel universe, I look at her curiously. "Then how do you know his name?"

She shrugs. "Heard about him but never spoken to him. He keeps himself to himself and that's fine by me."

I can't stop digging for information and say with interest. "So, um… what have you heard?"

She cuts another piece of cake and pushes it towards me. Maybe I can just live on this, it wouldn't be a hardship.

I listen as she tells me what she knows. "Word is, he's some big shot record producer. Then again, someone else said he was a movie star. Anyway, whatever he is, he doesn't do much. Just plays around on his boat and motorbike. He has a jet ski as well and a sports car. I guess he likes his toys."

I feel fascinated and dig a little deeper. "Does he have any family?"

She shrugs. Not that I know about. He has a different girl on his arm when he heads out of an evening but that's all I know. He doesn't mix with the locals and just hides away in his beach house."

She shrugs and starts clearing the plates away which just involves shifting them from the clear counter to sit on top of several other dishes.

I smile gratefully and say lightly, "Anyway, I shouldn't take up any more of your time. It's good to meet you, Sally. My door is always open as they say, so pop round anytime."

She walks me to the door and smiles. "Sure, thanks. See you around."

As I head down her path, I laugh to myself. Sally's an odd one that's for sure. I like her though.

Feeling quite upbeat, I carry on to Bert and Sheila's house. It takes me all of ten minutes to find and I see a pretty well-tended garden sprawling around a sweet little bungalow. My heart leaps. Yes, this is more like it. Normal life resumes.

I make my way to the door and note the polished step and immaculately kept lawn. They are obviously people after my own heart. Finally, I can have an adult conversation with intelligent people. Hurray for Bert and Sheila.

I ring their doorbell and hear it chime throughout the house. I don't have to wait long before a woman throws open the door, dusting flour from her hands and beaming broadly. "You must be Rachel. Come on in love, Bert's in the shed but I'll call him."

Happily, I follow her into the pristine bungalow and feel my world right itself. I'm pretty sure they must have a working shower here so maybe I can ask to use it once a week or something.

Sheila opens the back door and yells, "Bert, visitor!"

Then she turns and smiles. "So, it's lovely to meet you. I must say we were all a little worried when Molly took that nasty fall. Nobody knew what would become of the place but when they said they were renting it to a young lady, we were quite surprised. What's a pretty young thing like you doing hiding herself away out here?"

I squirm a little under her sharp gaze and say lightly, "I just needed to get away from my cheating fiancé. You know the sort, Sheila. I came where he wouldn't think to look for me."

Immediately, Sheila looks angry on my behalf. "I thought as much, it's always a man in my opinion. Well, if he comes here, I'll tell him a thing or two. You did the right thing love, keep away from men like that, they'll be trouble for the rest of your life if you let them."

Her husband makes his way inside and I see a kind looking elderly gentleman who smiles at me warmly. "You must be Rachel. Pleased to meet you, love. Now don't listen to Sheila here, she talks a lot of old wives' tales."

He pats her on the shoulder and she pretends to frown but doesn't quite pull it off. I laugh as I see the genuine love they have for each other which does restore my faith a little.

Sheila busies herself with making a pot of tea and fusses around me. "Sit down and tell me all about yourself. Do you work, where are you from, what did that man of yours do? Oh, I need to know everything."

Bert rolls his eyes and I stifle a giggle. I decided to skirt around the truth a little and just tell them I'm from London and work in the city at Viking foods. They look impressed and Bert says, "This must seem a little strange here. I mean, you're used to living in the fast lane. Here, it's not so much the slow lane more like the hard shoulder."

Sheila nods. "Yes, we've only just got broadband. The nearest supermarket is ten miles away and the only shops are in Pembury which isn't exactly convenient."

"It sounds like paradise to me," I say, meaning every word.

"London is busy, bustling and terrifying. Nobody has time for anyone else and the only objective is making money. I searched for a place that has none of its qualities, so I'm happy to hear your description of Perivale."

Bert nods. "You know, we haven't always lived here. Much like you we worked hard and had little spare time. When we retired, we came here with the sole aim of easing off the pedal a little. It suits us and brings the family to visit a few times a year. All that really matters is enjoying life as best you can and making the ends meet in the middle."

Sheila nods in agreement. "If you need anything just ask. We're always here unless we take the car to Pembury. Bert has his birdwatching and I attend the local bridge club. Do you play bridge, Rachel?

I shake my head. "No, but I'd like to try."

Sheila looks pleased. "Then be my guest at our next gathering. You can observe and see if it's your cup of tea."

I'm pretty sure I outstay my welcome but sitting in their warm cosy kitchen feels so good. They provide me with endless tea and gossip and if I could stay here all night, I would. Then I remember my date, for want of a better word and decide to head back.

After promising to visit often, I head back down the lane to Bluebell cottage.

♥4

Ok, I'm nervous and think I'm about to have a panic attack. I can't believe I've agreed to this, especially with a man who completely rubs me up the wrong way. I still can't get over his stupid name. Logan Rivers, that's a made-up name if ever I heard one.

Clothes go flying as I struggle to find anything worthy of being described as impressive. I hardly packed to dress up and go on a date my first day. What was I thinking?

So much for my new start, I may have to move on quicker than I thought if tonight goes how I think it will. Stupid Logan Rivers and his love of fast toys. Why did I ever agree to this? Maybe I should have offered him the other benefit in kind. At least he'd be gone within the hour and I'd have had some fun along the way. Tonight, promises to be tedium personified, while I struggle to string a sentence together with Logan flaming Rivers.

The only thing that passes as impressive in my whole suitcase is a white dress that falls to just above my knee. It's pretty basic but if I team it with some silver jewellery and a contrasting clutch bag and shoes, it may just pass the test. The only coat I brought with me is my ski jacket, so I resort to grabbing my pale blue pashmina and hope it's up to the job. The evenings are still a little cool and knowing him he's brought his stupid bike.

I still can't get used to seeing myself with blonde hair. I keep on catching sight of it in the mirror and think there's an intruder standing behind me. However, I do quite like the new me. I was due a change although I had just meant it to be my hair colour and not the whole of my life.

At 7.30 on the dot, according to my iPhone, I hear the rumble of a car's engine drawing up outside. I relax a little knowing it's not his bike. Then the nerves wash over me again and I start to hyperventilate. What am I doing? I'm such an idiot. This day is one of the weirdest in my life and yet something inside me is more alive than I've ever been. I am doing the unthinkable. Going where I never have before and through that door is the hottest man I've ever met, come to date *me*!

The sharp knock on the door reminds me what an asshole he is so, I set my mood accordingly and fling the door open with a bravado that deserts me the minute I lay eyes on him.

Logan looks me up and down and once again I feel naked. His eyes travel the length of me in a split second and leave me feeling open and exposed. He meanwhile, looks even hotter than earlier if that's possible. He is wearing smart chinos with a white shirt that's slightly open revealing his broad, tanned, chest. His eyes sparkle with amusement as he catches me staring and says roughly, "Good, you're on time. We don't have long and the last thing I needed was someone who kept me waiting."

He turns to leave, expecting me to follow dutifully behind which instantly gets my back up. So, I say quickly, "Sorry, you know us ladies, there's always something we've forgotten. Don't worry, I won't keep you waiting long."

Then I slam the door and lean against it laughing to myself. Take that creep face. He only needs to open that heavenly mouth of his and the words that come out irritate me beyond belief. He certainly never graduated from charm school so maybe he needs teaching some manners.

I decided to paint my nails while I make him wait. That should sufficiently get the message across. What a weirdo.

I think I've just managed one coat before the door opens and he storms in looking angry. He sees me sitting there and growls, "So, you forgot to paint your nails. Big deal. You know, I had you down as something more than the usual airheads I date. It looks like I got that wrong."

He marches over and sits before me, staring at me with a hard expression. I'm not sure why but seeing him here in this little cottage makes him seem even larger if that's possible. I try not to let him get to me and just carry on with my task but it's difficult when he is glaring at me so angrily.

I blow my nails to dry them and say sweetly. "You know, you really should take a chill pill. You'll have terrible medical problems if you let yourself get so wound up over such a trivial thing."

He raises his eyes and smirks. "So, you're a doctor now."

I smile knowledgeably. "Well, I could have been. I mean, I certainly got the grades. However, I couldn't face dealing with arrogant assholes every day so shelved that idea."

He laughs. "Arrogant assholes, in nursing?"

I blow my other hand. "No, surgeons. You see, my fun-loving friend, I could have been a brain surgeon if I wished. In fact, they begged me but I had to let them down gently. So, you see, I am sort of qualified to pass my diagnosis in a roundabout way."

He shakes his head. "Well, that's a big loss to the medical profession. No wonder the NHS is in dire straits."

Standing up, I smooth down my dress and note the sudden sparkle in his eyes as he watches me. What can I say, I'm a woman after all and am enjoying the sudden power I'm holding over him? Making sure I walk with my best wiggle forward, I say sharply. "Well, are you just going to sit there all night or do we have a function to attend?"

He rolls his eyes and follows me out and when I see what's waiting this time, I'm speechless. Parked outside the battered picket fence is a bright red Ferrari. I can almost feel his smirk from here as I stare at it in wonder. Spinning around, I say breathlessly, "Wow, I can't believe it. The FERRARI F50 screaming Banshee! I can't believe you have one. I thought there were only 349 ever made. How come you have one?"

Logan looks at me with amazement. "You know your Ferraris, how come?"

I say with excitement. "My father loved them. He always wanted one, and we used to spend hours researching them and going to local exhibitions. He taught me everything I know and he would be so excited to see this one up close."

I approach the car and say reverently, "May I?"

He nods and I stroke the gleaming paintwork of the supercar and commit it to memory. I take in every detail and almost salivate at the thought of riding in it. Quickly, I take out my phone and take a picture. Then I take a selfie of me next to it as Logan laughs. "You're a geek, do you know that?"

I grin. "Says the man who can't seem to buy something that isn't super powerful. What's wrong with a plain old Ford, anyway?"

He laughs and takes the phone from my hand.

"Here, let me take one of you at the wheel."

I drop the act pretty darned quickly when faced with this treat and gush, "Oh my god, can I? That would be amazing. I'll send it to my dad. He won't believe it."

Logan smiles and this time I see it's more relaxed. He loves this car that's obvious and is enjoying my reaction to it. He takes photos of me from every angle and as he joins me inside takes great delight in pointing out every inch of this gorgeous car. I clap my hands as he starts the engine and we share a smile as the car moves away. As I lean back against the seat, I savour the feeling of power beneath me. This car, like its owner, is impressive and I can't even begin to pretend I'm not impressed.

The ice appears to have melted and we chat about the car for most of the journey. I tell him about my father and he listens with interest. Then it dawns on me that I still don't know where we're going and say lightly, "So, what's the plan?"

I see his knuckles tighten on the steering wheel and feel the tension in the air as he sighs heavily. "Christopher Masters dinner party. He's a local businessman who calls the shots around here. I've been asked to his little gathering probably because he's looking for investors for his new golf course. The trouble is, I can't stand the man and golf even more."

I shake my head. "Then why are you going? You could have said no."

He shakes his head. "Not worth the trouble. No, it's just best to turn up, listen to his plan and then make up some excuse why I can't invest."

It falls silent until I say nervously, "What do you do exactly, Logan? I mean, the word is you're a movie star or a rock star. Which one is it?"

He laughs loudly, and the tension evaporates almost immediately.

"Where did you hear that?"

I shake my head. "Around."

"Well, for your information it's neither of the above."

"So, what is it then? I need to know if anyone asks me. I'll look a complete bozo if I don't even know your occupation."

He nods. "Ok, I design computer games."

Well, I wasn't expecting that and say with interest, "You must do very well at it."

He nods. "I do as it happens. I design the programmes and auction them out to the highest bidder. Apparently, my stuff sells well so the bids are quite high."

This is interesting and I long to know more but then he says casually, "So, what do you do to earn a living?"

His words bring back a subject I don't want to dwell on and I say sadly, "Oh, the usual. An administrative job in the city, completely dull and uninteresting and nothing like what you describe."

He won't give up.

"So, why are you here? An extended vacation or did they fire you?"

The pride in me rears its ugly head and I snap, "For your information, I was definitely not fired. Actually, I walked out and told them I was taking some time off. I'm certainly owed it so I'd like to see anyone argue with me. Also, the reason I had to get away so quickly was that I discovered my two-timing, asshole of a fiancé, was cheating on me with a bimbo called Camilla. Rather than face him, I ran, and that run brought me to Perivale. Does that answer your question?"

Once again, the silence falls and I take a few deep, calming, breaths.

Then he says softly, "The guys a fool."

Shaking my head, I say sadly, "No, Logan, I was the fool. I can see that now. I believed every lie he told me and did whatever he asked. I was so scared of losing him I became his puppet. It's only with the distance between us I can see how futile my efforts were. I was chasing something that was never really there in the first place. I had to get away for my own sanity and have a lot to think about before my time is up and I'm forced back to London."

Logan says harshly, "Why do you have to go back? You could start again somewhere else. There must be something you could do. I mean, an ex would be doctor and obvious gymnast like yourself."

I nod. "I can do anything, Logan, because I'm that sort of person. If I want to stay here, I will and nobody can persuade me otherwise. But I have a life back there. A home, family, friends, to name but a few. It's not that easy just to up sticks one day and never go back, no matter how much I want to."

He turns into a driveway and I look at the house nestling at the end of it with interest.

It's lit up with attractive outdoor lighting and many cars are already parked in every available space. I can't see any room left for the Ferrari and laugh softly. "Didn't think this one through, did you? I'm guessing you won't want to park your beloved on the street."

Logan snarls. "You're right. No, I'll just leave it right outside his front door. If anyone wants to leave, I'll move it."

He pulls up adjacent to the door and grins. "Shall we?"

I laugh as he jumps out and opens my door gallantly, offering me his arm.

As I take it, I sense a shift in our relationship as we walk inside the party as firm friends.

♥5

We are greeted by the sort of man I detest. The usual type I meet at the endless meetings I'm drafted into. Christopher Masters is one of them. He is fairly large, speaking of overindulgence and lack of exercise, rather than big bones as my mother would say. He has that supercilious air of a man who has success and elevates himself above the rest of society as a result. The sort of man who talks but never listens and ridicules rather than understands. I shiver inside as he greets Logan like a long-lost friend.

"Logan, my good chap, it's good to see you."

He merely glances in my direction and obviously files me under 'current bimbo' status, as he places his arm around Logan's shoulder and guides him into a drawing room filled with his own kind.

"Look who I found," he booms and several pairs of eyes turn in our direction and I shiver inside. Now I know why Logan was dreading coming.

Logan reaches out and pulls me close to his side and says icily, "I don't think you've met my companion, Rachel."

Christopher smiles at me pompously while his gaze rakes me from head to toe and strips me bare. He almost leers as he throws Logan *that* look. You know the one men use when they approve of the man's choice. Gritting my teeth, I just smile politely. "I'm pleased to meet you, Mr Masters."

He laughs jovially. "Call me Christopher, my dear. Now, let me offer you both a drink, is champagne good enough?"

Logan says dully, "Not for me, I'm driving. Soda water will be fine."

Christopher looks across to a young girl standing awkwardly in the corner. "Miriam, fetch our guest's soda water and a glass of champagne."

I stifle the irritation. No please, no thank you, just an order from an increasingly annoying man.

As she hurries off, Christopher whispers, "Got to train them young. She would make a good little wife for any man my Miriam."

I almost laugh as I see the meaning in his eyes. I'm pretty sure if this was Jane Austen's day, he would be making sure of a match made with my surly friend and his daughter. Goodness, this place really is behind the times.

Logan smiles but I can see his eyes have already glazed over.

An elegant lady comes over and smiles politely. I look at her with interest as she says in a clipped voice, "Logan, it's good to see you. Please introduce your charming companion."

Once again, I can't believe these people. Don't they think I can speak for myself? Before he can introduce me, I hold out my hand and say firmly, "I'm Rachel. I'm sorry, I didn't catch your name."

Looking a little taken aback the woman says haughtily, "Sophia Masters. The lady of the house."

My smile freezes in place as I sense Logan's amusement. Taking the limp-wristed hand of a woman who obviously hates physical contact, I make sure to grasp it hard and shake it vigorously. I take great delight in watching her wince and then really give them what they expect.

"Wow, Sophia, this place is amazing. I'm loving what you've done with it. So, period. I mean, you've really embraced the theme. I'm not going to lie; it takes a brave woman to stick to her guns in the face of popular trends. Good for you."

Christopher throws his wife a sharp look as she says tightly, "Thank you, my dear, compliment accepted. Now I must mingle with the other guests."

She heads off as quickly as she came and I throw Logan a triumphant look as he stifles a grin. Miriam arrives back with the drinks and I feel sorry as her hands shake as she hands Logan his soda. He thanks her and I watch her cheeks turn red and her eyes looking anywhere but him. Oh no, the poor girl. She's obviously holding a huge torch for him and I feel for her. She turns to me and offers me the champagne and I smile warmly. "Thank you so much, Miriam."

She smiles shyly and I whisper, "You'll have to look out for me tonight. I don't know anyone and it's all a bit scary."

She relaxes slightly and says in a gentle voice, "It is a bit. What do you want to know?"

Looking around, I see several people chatting in groups but turn to her and say softly. "Well, what about you? Tell me about yourself."

She looks surprised. "What... me?"

I nod as she laughs nervously. "There's not much to say really. You've met my parents and I've just finished university."

I say with interest, "What were you studying?"

I see the spark in her eyes as she returns to a comfortable subject. "Maths."

"You must be clever to study Maths, what do you want to do with it?"

She shrugs and says sadly, "If it were up to me, I'd travel a bit. You know, help out abroad, maybe as a nanny so I could learn a language or just go backpacking."

I look surprised. "Why don't you then?"

She rolls her eyes. "My father wants me to start at his company next week. They need a bookkeeper and apparently, I'll do."

"You'll do!"

She nods miserably. "Yes, he's told me I need to earn my keep and contribute to the family business. I'm to start in the accounts department and work there until I marry."

I look across and see her father laughing loudly and actually claps Logan on the back and I shudder. Turning to Miriam I say tightly, "Why don't you tell them what you'd rather do? I'm sure they'll help you and put the apprenticeship on hold."

Miriam looks dejected. "I'm not stupid, Rachel. It's not even worth raising the subject. No, it's best if I just do as they say and wait for the day I can leave and make my own life without them dictating it."

We hear a sharp, "Miriam, Mrs Carstairs needs a refill."

Looking over, I see the disapproving stare of Sophia directed at us and Miriam sighs. "Sorry, Rachel. I should tend to their guests."

As she scurries away, I feel sad for her. The product of years of being manipulated by overbearing parents. I don't blame her for being the way she is, she never stood a chance.

Logan comes over and whispers, "Kill me now."

I grin wickedly, "With pleasure but not before I've done away with our hosts."

He rolls his eyes. "I told you."

Suddenly, we hear a loud, "Dinner is served, please follow us into the dining room."

I shake my head in disbelief. "This is all a bit last century, isn't it? Who are these people?"

Logan laughs and offers me his arm. "Shall we, my dear?"

I take it and smile shyly, "If you wish oh master."

His eyes flash as he says darkly, "Careful, I'm quite liking this image."

Quickly, I draw my arm from his and say harshly, "In your dreams. Come on, I'm hungry enough to eat Sophia at this rate. She may not be safe from my cutlery."

Shaking his head, he follows me in.

As expected, dinner is a tedious affair. I'm seated between Logan on one side and an obnoxious man called Geoffrey, who keeps on spitting as he talks and making loud jokes that aren't funny. The only time he speaks to me is to patronise me as he points scores in front of his friends. Logan has Miriam on his other side and her father next to her. Christopher monopolises Logan's attention and makes sure to refer to his daughter at every opportunity. As the evening wears on she looks more and more mortified as her father's meaning becomes clear. He is trying, not so cleverly, to hook up his offspring with the very rich man beside her.

Logan is trying to be polite but I suspect it's out of respect for Miriam rather than her father.

After a while, I just sit silently and listen, hoping that time speeds up a little and we can make our escape. I'm actually exhausted because quite frankly this day doesn't appear to want to end. All I want is to wrap Bluebell cottage around me like a comfy blanket and sleep for the next week.

The conversation soon turns to the real reason for the invite and I listen with interest as Christopher outlines his plans for the new golf club.

He's obviously extremely proud of it and pontificates about how amazing it will be, how exclusive and nothing like this area has ever seen before.

Geoffrey appears interested and says loudly, "Sounds amazing, Masters. How much are you looking for investors to contribute?"

Christopher's eyes gleam as he goes in for the kill. "Good question, Geoffrey. You see, I only want to partner with people I can trust. Like-minded individuals who will relish the opportunity I'm giving them. The amount I need from four partners is £250,000 each."

The table falls silent, and he looks around with animation.

"I can tell you're surprised. You probably can't believe it's so cheap. Well, that's what's so good about it. £250K for a share in multi-million-pound golf and country club that's guaranteed to pay dividends before the first year's accounts are in. What can I say, I'm giving it away?"

Sophia smiles graciously and nods almost to reinforce his words.

Logan remains silent along with most of the other invited guests and Christopher talks loudly to cover it.

"So, I'm guessing I can count on your full support, I mean, you're not going to get an offer this lucrative ever again. The plans are in their final stage and permission is due to be granted early next month. Then we can get the bulldozers in and start creating my dream."

Geoffrey spits some food out as he says, "What if you don't get permission?"

Christopher looks around smugly, "I will because my college chum Tinky Witherspoon is the chairman of the planning committee. We were in the same house so those bonds never break. I don't foresee any obstacles in our way."

Sophia says lightly, "Christopher, we must raise a toast to our joint venture. I'm sure we are all in agreement that this is a solid investment."

Almost with relief the guests grab their glasses and toast the new venture but looking around at the faces of their guests, I'm thinking the only excitement for it is coming from our hosts.

When the meal ends, I can't get away fast enough. As evenings go that one was excruciating. It was everything I hate and came here to avoid. So much for getting away from it all.

Logan's quiet on the drive home and I'm not in the mood to make small talk. After a while, he sighs heavily and says apologetically. "I'm sorry, Rachel, your first night and it's with the likes of them."

I laugh softly. "It's fine. I wanted to get to know the locals, so that's a plus. Whether I want to see them again is out for debate, although, I did kind of like Miriam."

Laughing I tease, "I think Christopher's got plans for you two."

Logan groans. "Poor kid. She doesn't stand a chance with those two as parents. If I were her, I'd do a Rachel and disappear."

He grins and I have to laugh. "Maybe we could swap. She could go back to London and I'll stay here. She'll probably be better at putting up with Spencer than I am. I mean, years of dealing with her parents have set her up for life in being able to deal with insufferable, egotistical, self-absorbed, assholes."

Logan laughs. "You make your life sound so appealing."

I say gloomily, "My life's great on paper but the reality is very different. What is life, Logan? We are taught from an early age that success is measured in material possessions. We are steered along the path of a good job, owning our own home and providing for our future. Our success is measured in how high we climb that corporate ladder and how big our house is. Does the car we drive measure up to our neighbours and do our children go to the best schools? Is that really what life is meant to be? I mean, take Sally, my new neighbour. She appears to have nothing and lives quite frankly, in the untidiest house I have ever seen. To the real world, she's losing at life. She has nothing and hides away in solitude and deserves pity rather than praise. She wears the strangest clothes and looks as if she could do with a complete makeover. Her only friend is her cat, and she spends the day baking amazing cakes and painting anything that catches her eye. Well, I think she's got it right. She owes nobody anything and asks for nothing in return. She pleases herself and does what makes her happy."

Logan says softly, "How do you know she's happy?"

For a moment I can't answer him. The question hangs in the air and can't connect with an answer.

I say in a small voice. "I don't. I've only met her once, but she seems happy enough."

Logan says wistfully. "We're all the same, Rachel. We see what's in front of us and judge before knowing the facts, its human nature. You saw your neighbour and because you're unhappy with your life you saw someone who appeared to have it all worked out. For all you know, Sally's story could be similar to yours. She may be running from something and hiding away to prevent having to deal with it. Take me for instance. This evening was a case in point. Christopher Masters sees my expensive toys and seemingly wealthy life. He sees a man with money to spare who's a little rough around the edges, who wouldn't question his investment because it's obvious he knows nothing about business."

I say with surprise. "Why would he think you know nothing about business? You must know a lot to be able to afford your lifestyle."

He laughs. "Because men like that don't live in today's world. They don't see this new generation of people earning vast sums of money from the internet. They don't understand how this world operates and think it's just people getting lucky and will soon pass. Men like him are dinosaurs and not open to change. He'll think I'm an easy touch and probably grateful for the chance to join the big boys. Well, I'm not. I just want to do what I love and enjoy the life I want to lead. I don't want to partner anyone because I'm selfish and only want to please myself. I don't want to build a business and be responsible for other people's lives. The thought of working in an office and attending board meetings leaves me cold. That's my life, Rachel, you see, I'm every bit the asshole you thought I was."

The car stops and I look out in surprise to see we're already back at Bluebell cottage. Logan smiles. "Here you go, one favour repaid and one grateful recipient. I'm sorry your evening was probably the worst you've ever had but I'm grateful. Well, it was a pleasure to meet you and anytime you need a helping hand or just want to hang out, you know where I am."

I smile and raise my eyes. "No, I don't."

He shakes his head, "Don't what?"

"Know where you are. I mean, you came out of nowhere and then disappeared as fast. I know you have a beach house but I wouldn't know where. Not that I'm some crazy stalker or anything, who would spy on you as soon as I know where you live, but being new in town I could sure use a friend to pester once in a while."

For a second, our eyes meet. Logan stares at me with the look of someone who is working out his options. I can see every question in his eyes and watch as he reasons with himself. Whatever this connection we've made is, neither one of us know what to do about it. There's an attraction there, but it's not the right time to act on it. Could we be friends? Probably. Should we be friends? Probably not because I've got a feeling being friends with this man would be complicated for my heart.

He obviously reaches a decision because he smiles and his eyes flash. "Well, Rachel. Today has been intriguing. If it's ok with you I'd like to show you around. I have a feeling you may need someone to guide you away from the perilous mistakes you are sure to make and someone who worries that you're not safe to be allowed out alone."

He laughs as I roll my eyes and takes my hand and kisses it gallantly. "Good luck settling in. I'm away for a few days but when I return, I'll stop by and make good on my promise. Try to stay out of trouble until then."

Snatching my hand away, I pretend to be annoyed. "For your information, I can look after myself and don't need a man to save me from anything. However, I recognise that being the person you are, you need all the friends you can get, so, yes, I will allow you to show me around out of kindness for the needy."

He shakes his head as I try to exit as gracefully as a sports car will allow me to and I feel him watching me as I head through the rusty gate of home and am safely inside. As I hear the car start up and pull away, I sigh inside. Logan Rivers has complicated an already extremely complicated situation. This wasn't supposed to happen and yet when I heard that car drive into the darkness, I find myself counting the days until I see him again.

♥6

When I wake up, at first, I wonder where I am. However, it doesn't take long before it all comes flooding back and I lie in shock for a while. I really did this. I really left everything behind and started again.

As I look at the unfamiliar surroundings, I feel at peace with myself. There is no anxiety, no worries and no blind panic at what I've done. The only thing I feel now is excitement.

Grinning to myself, I wonder how my email went down. There will be anger as Spencer tries every trick in the book to find me. Because if I'm sure of anything, it's that. Spencer Scott will be out of his mind with worry right about now and it couldn't happen to a more deserving person.

I stretch out in the double bed that I have all to myself and savour the feeling. The sun is peeking through a crack in the lovingly handmade curtains, reminding me I have slept in for once. Usually, I would have been up hours ago. I always wake in the darkness and fall asleep in the darkness. Not anymore. Now I can lie in bed all day if I want to and it feels liberating.

If I had a working one, I would be heading to the shower right about now but instead, I swing my legs to the side of the bed and search for my slippers. The bare boards are cool to the touch and although probably an excellent exfoliator for my feet, I would actually prefer the comfort they offer rather than the cold, hard, floor.

Stretching, I listen to the birds singing outside and smile to myself. As the memories surface of my first day here, I feel a warm glow of excitement as I think of Logan and our date last night.

The man fascinates me. He's so brusque, charmless and surly, yet underneath has a soft side that intrigues me. There is more to that man than meets the eye and I'm looking forward to seeing him again. I never did ask him where he was going because why would I? I don't need to know his diary and wouldn't expect to tell him mine. The fact mine is now a blank sheet of paper fills me with an alien sense of freedom and I must say it feels good.

I decide to have some breakfast and manage to rustle up a bowl of cereal and some toast from the meagre rations I brought with me. Maybe I should head to Pembury today to stock up.

As it's such a beautiful morning, I decide to sit on the rusty bench and enjoy my breakfast in the garden. A rare treat that I value above anything Saracens could offer.

As I sit enjoying the peace and quiet, I hear the noise of machinery coming from across the road. Looking over, I see a man pushing a lawnmower around Sally's small garden and watch him with interest.

As gardeners go, he's easy on the eye. Tall, tanned and made of muscles. His hair is fair and cut short and he's wearing a white t-shirt and cut-off jeans. Shaking my head, I wonder about this place. Perivale appears to be overrun by hot guys and I'm not complaining.

Feeling a little self-conscious in my pyjamas, I head back inside and watch him from the window instead. From my vantage point behind the curtains, I stare at his rippling muscles. Then I stare at the way his blue eyes sparkle even from across the road and sigh at the competent way he handles his machine. Eye candy of the best kind and all that's missing is the sight of him downing a bottle of Evian and spilling it all over his tight-fitting t-shirt.

Feeling slightly disturbed by my own thoughts, I move away from the hot guy and try to concentrate on the not so hot mess looking back at me through the cracked mirror.

Sighing, I fill the sink with another bowl of water and prepare to re-live turn of the century bathing.

Once I'm semi-presentable, I set about unpacking. I may as well make the place feel like home and so try to organise my things around me. It seems strange seeing familiar objects among unfamiliar ones. The latest lotions and potions sit on tarnished shelves. Designer outfits hang in antique wardrobes and expensive jewellery is placed carefully in dusty, wooden, drawers that appear to stick shut.

It doesn't take me long to place the new among the old and despite everything I love this place as if it's a palace.

Deciding to locate the cleaning items, I set about poking around in the kitchen cupboards with a view to giving the place a sparkle clean.

I think I've only found half an empty bottle of washing up liquid and a threadbare cloth before I hear a knock on the door.

Feeling slightly hopeful that Logan is here to say his goodbyes, I fling the door open revealing the other hot guy in town. Lawnmower man.

The sun blinds me for a minute and when I refocus, I see the man smiling at me with one of *those* looks. You know, the one that sets the housewives heart on fire and gives meaning to their day. His eyes sparkle as he says cheerfully, "Hi, you must be Rachel. I'm Jack, the handyman around here."

Smiling a little self-consciously, I say in a slightly breathless voice, "Oh, um… hi… Jack. Yes, I'm Rachel, I'm pleased to meet you."

He winks and I stare. I do try not to but he is so gorgeous. Maybe it's because I'm out of my comfort zone but suddenly my mind has become some sort of man radar. It zones in on a welcome smile and a hot look. This isn't like me so I try to get it together and say politely. "How can I help you, Jack?"

He smiles. "Actually, I think I can help you. The owners of Bluebell cottage have asked me to sort out a shower for you. Apparently, it was meant to have been done before the place was rented. I'm sorry you've had to wait but I can start today if that's convenient."

Just for a second, I look past him and check that I'm actually still on earth and not in some parallel universe where only dreams come true or failing that, heaven.

Maybe I died in a crash on the way here and this is utopia. Then I realise my vision of paradise would have been a state-of-the-art bathroom from the word go, so I smile with relief and fling the door open as wide as it can go.

"Of course, it's convenient. Even if it wasn't, I'd alter my plans. You actually don't know how glad I am to see you."

He laughs and follows me inside and looks around with a little sadness. "I was sorry to hear about Molly, she's a lovely lady and the thought of her in a care home is a little upsetting."

I nod. "It must be terrible for her. I mean, look at what she's left behind. This place is paradise."

Jack laughs. "Not quite but it could be. Let me take a look at the bathroom and I'll get started on restoring the 21st century in here."

Trying hard not to follow him close behind into the small, cramped, bathroom, I say instead, "Would you like a cup of tea or coffee?"

He shouts over his shoulder, "Tea thanks. Milk, one sugar."

Thankful for the distraction, I set about making the drink. Almost as soon as the tea is made, he heads back and runs his fingers through his slightly spiky hair. "This may take longer than I thought. I need to rip out the bath and replace it with a new one complete with shower attachment. They didn't tell me it was so far gone; I'm just amazed they let it go so badly."

I nod. "Yes, poor Molly. She must have had a hard time with that bath."

Jack shrugs. "She was probably used to it. Sometimes you don't miss what you never had in the first place. I'm guessing she just adapted to things as they became less serviceable. I see it all the time. Dripping taps that have driven their owners mad for months when all it takes is a washer and ten minutes of time to fix. Peeling paintwork that's soon restored with just a few hours of hard work. People carry on with their lives but often don't see what's in front of them. If they do, they don't see the solution. This is no different. It probably never even crossed Molly's mind to change it. She just adapted and made the best of what she had."

He takes the mug I offer him and takes a swig of the tea, smiling gratefully. I'm left to fixate on the sight of his lips wrapping around the delicate bone china mug and salivating at the ripple of his muscles as he moves across to the window.

He looks outside and appears thoughtful. "You know, this place has such a fantastic view. I've always loved it. This is the real value of this property. It may need a few repairs but that view will never tarnish or get old. You are lucky to wake up to this every day."

I stare at him with interest. "Where do you live, Jack?"

He smiles. "Pembury. I live in a small cottage near the school. I'm quite proud of it because it's the first home I've owned, and I saved up for years for the deposit."

He looks so proud it makes me smile and he looks at me with interest. "What brought you here?"

I shrug and say sadly, "Life just got a little too heavy, and I had to get away. You know, guy trouble and I'm working out what to do about it."

He says thoughtfully, "You shouldn't let a guy drive you out of town. If I were you, I'd have stayed and let him have it."

Laughing, I raise my eyes, "And how would I do that?"

He grins wickedly, "Karate chops always work well, failing that buy a big dog and train it to attack. It's what he deserves, obviously."

"Obviously?"

"Well, obviously the guys a fool. I mean, anyone who could make a pretty girl cry must be. I'm probably guessing he didn't appreciate you while you were there and took it for granted that you always would be."

Trying to push away the thought that I now love this guy, I say with interest, "What about you? Do you have a girl you treat like a princess?"

He winks. "Only one and I'd do anything for her."

My heart sinks with disappointment and my head nods at him with appreciation, telling me, 'See, there are some good ones out there.'

Before I can ask him about her, he sets the mug down and starts towards the door. "Well, I'll head to town and pick up a new tub and shower. Don't worry if you need to go out, I can always come back later."

He sets off down the path and I shout, "Wait!"

He turns and looks at me with surprise and I say shyly, "I don't suppose I could hitch a ride? I need to grab some groceries and don't know where to go."

He nods. "Sure, jump in with me and I'll drop you to the store while I get the tub. Then I'll pick you up on my way past."

Grabbing my purse, I lock the door and happily jump into the passenger side of his truck.

♥7

Jack is good company as we head into town. He points out various landmarks along the way, alongside a potted history of Perivale. He paints a picture of a place I can't wait to get to know and I say with interest. "Have you lived here all your life?"

He nods. "Yes, some may say that's a bad thing, I'm not one of them."

I have to agree with him. "Why change something that's right from the start. I have moved around, Jack and let me tell you, nothing I've seen even comes close to this place."

He looks interested. "Where are you from?"

"London. I mean, that's where I live now but I was born in a town in Kent. My family still live there but I moved to London for work purposes."

He smiles sympathetically. "Bad luck."

I look at him with interest. "You say you're the local handyman. Well, I know you do plumbing and gardening, what other skills do you have?"

He raises his eyes and I blush a little as he winks. "I do anything that needs doing. I like to work with my hands and love the great outdoors."

A part of me is trying not to focus on those hands of his and imagine what they could do for me, so I say lightly, "Um... Sally's a lovely lady. Has she lived here long?"

Jack laughs. "Sally's great but she's hardly a lady."

I look at him in surprise. "Why?"

He shakes his head. "Sally may look older but she's a lot younger than you think."

"Why, how old is she?"

He sighs. "Must be in her early thirties. She hides away in that cottage from the world because she has no faith in it."

"How do you know?"

He smiles. "When people are lonely, they open up to a kind ear and a friendly smile."

I sit thinking about his words for a minute and then say, "How does she afford to live? I mean, I'm pretty sure you don't come cheap and the rent must cost her a bit."

He grins and for some reason, my heart jumps a little inside. "She pays me in kind."

Oh, for god's sake, that again, what is this place?

He laughs as he sees the look I give him. "She pays me in cake. I mean, have you ever tried it? That woman is a culinary genius, undiscovered like many of the fossils on the beach below her cottage."

I roll my eyes, "I'm not sure she would like being compared to a fossil."

Laughing, he throws me that look again, the one that makes me wonder if I need to seek help for hot guy addiction. What is this place messing with my libido when I should be considering swearing off men for life?

Coughing slightly, I try to change the subject,

"So, um… tell me about your girlfriend, or is she your wife?"

He laughs softly. "I never said I had one."

My heart jumps a little and I roll my eyes at it and beat it back down. I say in a rather high voice, "Oh, I'm sorry, it's just that you said you had a girl you would do anything for."

He laughs. "I was talking about Millie, my dog."

Why does the relief at his words threaten to drown my heart?

"Your dog?"

He smiles and I'm fascinated by the way his expression softens at the mention of her and his whole face lights up.

"Yes, she's a border terrier that I took in when her owner moved abroad. She's great company and I'm happy to have found her."

I can tell he obviously loves his faithful friend and smile as I say, "Where is she now?"

He grins. "Sally's. She also pays me by looking after Millie when I'm busy. She gets on well with her cat and adores Sally so it works out well. Sally helps me and I return the favour by doing her garden and fixing anything that needs it."

Then he turns and says with interest, "You know, if you're going to stick around, maybe you could try and get to know Sally a little. She doesn't have many people to talk to and could use a friend. I think you'll get on because once you get past her reservations, she's the funniest person I know and the kindest."

Once again, this place has surprised me. When I met her, I filed Sally away in my mind as a little eccentric and a woman who wanted to be left alone. Logan's words come to mind when he told me I had judged her at face value. Apparently, he was right and I feel a little ashamed of my blinkered view of life.

I don't even notice we've left the countryside behind until I see the fields have been replaced with buildings and busy roads. I look with interest at the small town opening up before me and Jack says, "This is Pembury. It's a little out of date but a great place to call home."

The buildings all appear a little dated and the people walking by appear to have more time than those in London. I see couples looking in shop windows or talking to others in the street. Tables and chairs are filled with people gossiping over a coffee rather than the usual Londoners marching down the streets holding their coffee to go as they charge from one tube station to the next. Women push prams and their laughter fills the air. The traffic is fairly busy but nothing like the noise and choking fumes of the ones in London. The sky is blue here rather than tainted by fumes and smog and the little shops that make up this town are obviously family run and not the usual chains that dominate the larger high streets.

Jack smiles as he pulls to a stop outside a large grocery store called Mulligans.

"Here you are, Rachel. Emma and Greg stock most of the things you'll need. If they don't, they'll soon get it for you."

I smile my thanks and he says, "I'll meet you back here in an hour. Have fun."

I watch him drive away and feel warm inside. Jack appears like most of the people I've met in this magical place. For some reason, out of everyone, he seems the most familiar to me. I feel as if I've known him all my life, and comfort surrounds me like a blanket as I imagine him picking me up later. Why does he seem so right?

♥8

Mulligans is a complete treasure trove. Rows upon rows of things you always need, sitting alongside the things you've never heard of or forgotten about. This place is fascinating and one hour just doesn't seem long enough.

Grabbing a wheelie basket, I head down the aisles looking with interest at the array of wares jostling for position on extremely crowded shelves.

I can't remember the last time I went grocery shopping. Usually I do it online and have it delivered at the same time every week. Everything is ordered for convenience and I never had time to experiment. Work is such a big part of my life that anything else gets put to the back of the queue. Maybe this will be a good time to discover if I can actually cook rather than just heat up ready meals or call Deliveroo.

The customers that walk with me are different to the people I usually mix with. Fashion has no place here, just practicality and whatever appears to hand. The people shopping in this colourful emporium do so with a smile on their face rather than the anxiety-ridden look of a person running out of time in their day. These people obviously have their priorities right because they don't appear as short tempered as your average busy executive grabbing a sandwich in Pret a Manger. No, these people have time, something I am beginning to discover the value of.

I see her looking at the magazines and do a double take. Cautiously I approach and whisper, "Miriam, isn't it?"

She jumps as if startled and looks around guiltily. I stifle a smile as she surreptitiously tries to hide the latest OK magazine.

She smiles shyly. "Hi, um… Rachel."

I nod and say, "I'm glad I ran into you, we never got to carry on our conversation yesterday."

Miriam looks around fearfully and whispers, "I'm sorry about last night, Rachel. Those dinner parties are excruciating. My parents can be… um… well… oh, I'm sure you know."

I smile sympathetically. "It's ok, you don't need to explain. I've met many like them before and definitely will again. I'm sure they meant well."

She shakes her head. "It's ok, you don't have to make excuses for them. I gave up doing that years ago. The trouble is, they'll never change. Everything's a business opportunity and they can't see beyond Pembury and the surrounding area."

I nod towards a coffee shop across the street. "Do you have time to grab a coffee with me? I could quickly buy what I need and treat you if you want to."

Miriam smiles but looks nervous. "I would love to but I'm expected back in ten minutes. It's my first day as the bookkeeper and the woman in charge is quite fearsome. I daren't be late back."

She laughs awkwardly and I feel a rush of resentment towards her father. So, I just shrug and say kindly, "No problem. We can always do it another time when you're free?"

She smiles sweetly. "I'd like that, it would be good to talk to someone normal for a change."

Laughing, I roll my eyes. "Trust me, Miriam, I'm far from normal."

As I turn to leave, she says quietly, "Out of interest, Rachel, did Mr Rivers say if he was going to invest or not?"

I look at her in surprise. "Why?"

She colours up a little and looks nervous again. I watch the panic enter her eyes as she blushes furiously.

"I'm sorry, I'm not asking for my father or anything like that. It's just that I was kind of hoping, well, that, um… he said no."

Before I can ask why, she looks at her watch and visibly pales. "Oh my god, I'm already late and it's my first day. Sorry, Rachel, I have to dash. It was good seeing you again."

I watch her almost sprint to the door leaving the magazine discarded on the shelf. Once again, I feel sorry for her. She's nervous of everything and I can only blame her parents. I wonder why she wanted Logan to turn them down though? Something in her expression has rung the alarm bells and I decide at the first possible opportunity I'll find out whatever it is she's hiding.

Once I've filled my little trolley basket, I wait patiently in line to pay.

The two people serving behind the counter are obviously in no hurry. They chatter away to each other as well as the customers they are serving. I listen to their friendly banter and smile. Familiarity sits alongside friendship. It's obvious these people all know each other. They talk about mutual friends and their laughter is genuine. I never knew people like this really existed and feel very happy I came.

My ears prick up as they start talking about one resident in particular.

"Hey, did you know Max is back?"

The woman serving looks excited.

"I heard he was due but didn't know when. How do you know?"

The lady in front of me says, "Maria told me. She had to give the place a once over yesterday. Apparently, he's heading this way tomorrow."

The man serving beside her, rolls his eyes. "Thanks for the warning. I'll spread the word to lock up your daughters."

The lady beside him openly sighs and he pretends to look annoyed. From their behaviour I guess they're the owners, Emma and Greg and Emma laughs. "Good luck with that. I'll expect him to bowl in here as usual and charm the customers."

The lady in front of me nods in agreement. "You know, if I was ten years younger, I'd be in there like a shot."

Greg raises his eyes and shoots his wife an amused look. I can see why because the woman in front must be well into her 80s. Emma nods. "Me too."

Greg really does frown now and I laugh along with the others. The older lady laughs, actually she giggles adorably. "You know, when I was a young girl, I was considered quite a catch down at the local dance. If a man like Max Summers was around then, I'm guessing I would have stood a very good chance."

Emma smiles sweetly. "I can see that, Connie. You've still got it."

Connie laughs happily. "I do inside and live it out in my dreams. The body may be old but the mind never ages."

Emma smiles as she places the last item in the shopping bag. "I can't agree with you more, Connie. I still feel 21."

Greg looks at her fondly. "You'll always be that young girl I married, Emma."

They share a look that only years of love and friendship creates. Watching them it reminds me of my own relationship and I can't remember Spencer ever looking at me like that. Usually, I get a quick peck on the cheek or a distracted hug. Spencer's always been so driven and races through the day like Usain Bolt. Any intimacies we share are usually in bed at night after a ready meal deal and a bottle of wine before setting the alarm clock and falling to sleep. A bitter feeling twists my heart as I feel cheated by him all over again. The way he was looking at Camilla was no different. He wanted something from her that he tolerated from me. Maybe he looked at me like that once when he was doing the chasing and on the charm offensive. It took me a while to trust him enough to let my guard down and into my life and then he spent the next year cementing our union by moving in and putting a ring on my finger. Everything was done like the proverbial text book.

Find a woman – check.

Sweep her off her feet and make her fall in love with you – check.

Make her believe that you're the one and slip a ring on her finger – check.

Move in and start calling the shots – check.

Undermine her self-confidence and make her worried you'll leave – check.

Take away her independence and alienate all her friends – check.

Become the only person she can trust and believe that she can't exist without you, then cheat on her continuously while making out it's her own paranoia and a product of her possessive imagination – check.

Go one step too far and destroy her….?

Feeling my heart harden, I crush that last one in the dust under my shoe. I refuse to allow him to destroy me. Spencer Scott has it coming and I just need this time to work out how.

Feeling a tap on my shoulder, I spin around and see Jack standing there. Once again, my heart jumps a little and right into his arms like the tart she is. He smiles that panty melting smile that promises so much devastation and says lightly, "All done. Mack will deliver it this afternoon and help me put it in place. I just need to disconnect the old one, so I'm afraid you'll be without water for the rest of the day."

We move up to the counter and Emma smiles happily. "Hey, Jack. Good to see you."

He smiles warmly. "Hey, guys, have you met Rachel, she's moved into Bluebell cottage?"

They smile politely and I see Emma's eyes flash with amusement, making me wonder if I put my t-shirt on backward or have lipstick on my cheek. She shares a look with Greg who smiles softly,

"Welcome, Rachel. We were sorry to hear about poor Molly, such a terrible thing to happen. I'm sure she'll be happy to know her cottage is in good hands though."

I smile warmly. "Thanks, Greg. I didn't know her but almost feel as if I do through her lovely possessions. What was she like?"

Emma smiles as she starts ringing up my purchases. "You know, Molly was one of a kind. A proud woman who always refused to let anything get her down. She had a hard life in some ways, lost her husband to a heart attack when he was only 50. She always worked and yet managed to find time to involve herself with every village event and organised most of them. Her kids were two of the most well-behaved ones in the village and she was someone you could always rely on for an interesting chat and to tell you what was going on. She will be sorely missed around here."

Jack nods. "Yes, we'll all miss Molly."

Once again, I feel a warmth spreading through me as I see the genuine love these people have for the woman whose life I've invaded. I live in her home, surrounded by her possessions. The only thing about to change is the rusty old bath tub and I feel sad that she never got the pleasure of it.

Greg laughs. "I'm guessing they don't know what's hit them at that care home she's probably controlling right about now. I'll say one thing for

Molly, she doesn't let anything get her down and will be making the best of it, you mark my words."

Emma nods and says cheerfully, "That will be £29.75, love."

Handing over my card, I'm surprised when Jack reaches over and grabs the bags. I'm not sure why but I like having him here. I like the fact he's helping me and a part of me wishes we were a couple like Greg and Emma who are obviously so happy together. I want that. I want someone who doesn't look at me with an impatient frown if I'm a few minutes late. I want someone who doesn't sigh with exasperation if I say something they don't agree with and I want someone who doesn't make me feel as if they're doing me a favour by giving me their precious time. I want that all-encompassing love that shuts the world out and unites two people as a team in every way. Two people who share everything, yet are free to pursue their dreams with only encouragement and pride from their partner. I want to feel loved and cherished and made to feel I count. Why does that appear to involve the man standing waiting patiently for me to pay?

Emma hands me my receipt and I don't miss the approval in her eyes as she looks between us. Like a proud mother she smiles at Jack and says cheerily, "Now don't be a stranger, Jack. We may need your help in fixing some broken tiles in the kitchen. Drop by when you get a chance and I'll show you."

Jack nods. "Consider it done, Emma."

They turn to the next customer after saying goodbye and I walk with Jack back to his truck. As we reach the door, I remember the conversation before he came in and say with interest, "Who's Max Summers? I overheard them saying he's back, and they seemed quite excited."

Jack rolls his eyes and grins. "Max owns that big house overlooking the bay not far from Bluebell cottage. He's not here much because he's a pilot but tries to come back a few times a year. I heard his family are staying for the school holidays. I doubt he'll be here that long though. He's very busy and especially in the Summer."

I nod. "Because it's holiday season?"

He nods. "Yes, he's always busy but more so in August. I expect he's here to make sure the house is ready for his family when the schools break up."

He puts the shopping in the back of his truck and smiles.

"So, let's head back and restore a little of Bluebell cottage to what it once was."

As he starts the engine, I say with interest, "Do you know Miriam Masters, Jack?"

He nods. "Yes, I've known her for years. Nice girl."

"Yes, she seems to be. I met her last night at a party her parents hosted. She's different to them, luckily."

He sighs. "Yes, thank God. Unfortunately for her they are two of the most obnoxious people you'll meet around here. They treat everyone as if they're beneath them and have no regard for normal life."

I laugh softly. "I saw that. Do you know much about this golf club he wants to build?"

Jack nods. "Yes, it's been in the planning for years. He's looking for investors to help build it and then he's going to sell membership to keep it running. I've heard it's going to be quite pricey, nothing many of the locals could afford."

"Then who'll join if the locals can't?"

He shakes his head. "Oh, he'll get his members. They'll come in from the neighbouring villages and towns. There isn't another golf club for miles so I'm sure he'll be busy."

Something still confuses me and I say hesitantly, "What if he doesn't get his backing? Will the project be shelved?"

Jack laughs loudly. "Oh, he'll get his money. Men like Christopher Masters always do. He's part of the old boy's network. They look after their own kind and don't care who they destroy in the process."

I detect a trace of bitterness in his voice and say softly, "Why do you say that?"

He shakes his head and sighs. "The plans take it across beautiful countryside. Currently it's given over to birds and wildlife and many locals enjoy the freedom of it. It sits among some of the best scenery in the area and I'm guessing that once Christopher gets the bulldozers in, a part of history will be gone forever. Don't get me wrong, I'm all for change and certainly Perivale could use some investment but it breaks my heart to see it. Maybe I'm selfish but I love going up there because it reminds me of what's important in life."

As his words hit me, I catch them and hold them to my heart. I have always thought change was good, inevitable and a necessary evil. However, now I've experienced a different kind of change, I feel protective of it. Then I say with alarm, "You say, Perivale. Will that affect our cottages?"

Jack shakes his head. "I don't think so. It will be close by but shouldn't affect you. I'd have known about it if it was."

Feeling slightly relieved, I sit back and enjoy the journey. This place, like the people I've met, is growing on me faster than I ever thought possible. I wonder what other surprises it has in store?

♥9

Jack helps me take the shopping inside and looks around him with a smile. "You know, Rachel. I used to come here as a kid. My mum loved a good gossip with Molly and helped out with all her planning committees. There was once an apple tree in the back garden I enjoyed climbing. If I was lucky, Molly would make us some apple pies and there was never a finer tasting one."

He shakes his head sadly. "The tree got diseased and had to be chopped down about two summers ago. It broke my heart because I was called in to do the honours. I remember Molly just smiling as she saw the felled tree at her feet and taking my hand. She squeezed it and said not to miss the past when the future promises so much more. She told me to hold it in my memory and be happy that at least I had that to cherish. Then she told me we would plant a new tree in the grave of the old. It would one day stand as proud as the one before it and give the future generations pleasure. She said it's just the circle of life and nothing lasts forever. The old makes way for the new and we shouldn't be sad about that."

He looks over and smiles and the sunlight catches it and warms my heart. I feel the tears welling up in my eyes and he laughs softly. "Now I've made you sad, and that wasn't my intention. I just wanted to share a little of the history of this place so you can understand its past."

He moves away from the window and smiles guiltily. "Anyway, I should get to work. I need to turn off the water, so if you need to fill a kettle or a few bowls of water, now is probably a good time to do it."

He heads off, and I set about filling whatever I can with water, his words haunting me as I work. Moving across to the window I see the small tree standing proudly and a little spark of hope ignites my soul. I can be that tree. I can face a new future and do it alone. So, what if the past didn't turn as I thought it would? I'm not finished by a long way and owe it to myself to take this fork in the road.

As the birds sing outside and the sun beats down on the weed strewn path, I make a vow to myself. This is my beginning. It may be the end of something but there's no time to dwell on the past when the future, like Molly said, is even more promising.

As Jack works away in the bathroom, I set about doing what I always intended to – clean the cottage.

It's such a lovely day that lights up every nook and cranny. Taking full advantage of it, I clean away the dust and wash the floors. I set aside a pile of washing to be done when the water comes back on and look around with delight at the fresh clean rooms sparkling at me in the sunshine. Yes, the furniture is old and scratched. The sofa looks a little threadbare, and the cushions lost their shape many years ago. The floor needs a good polish and the curtains a good clean but this place feels more like home than the flat I lived in with Spencer. The two are poles apart. One old, battered and loved, with few modern conveniences and luxuries. The other filled with state-of-the-art gadgets, a designer bathroom and chrome and mirrors framing the London skyline. As I look around, I realise that unlike Bluebell cottage, that place never really felt like home.

I make Jack some tea and smile as I hear him whistling along to the small radio he brought in from the truck. Leaning against the bathroom door, I shamelessly watch him working away, admiring the capable way he deals with things I have no understanding of. He catches my eye in the mirror and laughs. "Sorry, is the music too loud?"

Holding out the mug of tea, I shake my head. "No, it's fine. It brings life to the place. You know, Jack, I envy you."

He takes a sip of his tea and laughs. "Why?"

"Because you have such a great life here. You fit in and that's lovely to see."

He looks surprised. "I fit in, what does that mean?"

I shrug sadly. "This place suits you. You have a good job you love, a girl you would do anything for, friends and neighbours who obviously adore you and you get to live in Perivale and Pembury which must surely be paradise."

He laughs. "Well, put it like that, yes I do. So, tell me about Rachel. Why is her life so sad she thinks this is paradise?"

Gazing out of the small window I say sadly, "Because I don't have time."

He sounds surprised. "What, time to tell me?"

Looking back at him, I see the concern and just smile softly. "No, time to live. Time to enjoy the simple things in life and time to explore the obvious. We all take things for granted, Jack. The sky above our heads and the ground we walk on. The food we buy and the seasons that change. Usually, I notice none of them. I work from dawn 'til dusk and think I have a great life. I have it all, according to most and yet in my heart I have nothing."

He says gently, "Are you talking about the guy – you know, the fool?"

I grin. "No, not really. Some may say I'm the fool for putting up with him. In fact, the longer I stay here the clearer it becomes. I thought I loved him but I can see I never did. I was just fooling in love rather than falling. I was falling for an idea, a dream and an expectation. I thought I loved him and spent most days proving it to myself and him. The trouble is, I was that fool, Jack because I can see now, he never loved me. Not like Greg does Emma or Bert does Sheila. That's real love. You have it with Millie and Sally has it with Vixen. I need to start with myself and then maybe one day I'll be lucky enough to find someone to share it with."

I laugh as I see his expression. Poor guy, he must think I'm an idiot. Shaking myself, I smile happily. "Anyway, you don't want to hear my troubles. Maybe I'll head across the street to Sally and see if I can exchange some of that cake of hers for a favour – you know, pay her in kind."

Jack laughs. "It's the best payment there is. Go and check on my girl while you're at it. I think she'll love you."

Taking the empty mug from his hand, we share a smile and I can't wait to see where this new life of mine will take me.

♥10

Leaving the sanctuary of Bluebell cottage, I head across the street to Sally's. I actually feel a little self-conscious. Maybe she'd prefer to be left alone and will think I'm some sort of interfering busy body.

However, as soon as I raise a hand to knock on her battered door, it opens revealing her in all her glory. Today Sally is dressed in a light orange jumper and turquoise flowery trousers. Her hair is dyed white and her glasses are perched on her head showing her amazing green eyes that sparkle with amusement.

This Sally is very different to the first one I met, and she laughs as a little furry bundle almost knocks me flying.

"Down, Millie!"

Looking down, I see the gorgeous face of Millie, Jack's pride and joy and can't help but smile. Reaching down, I make to stroke her head but she jumps into my arms and starts licking my face vigorously. Sally laughs. "She likes you, Rachel. Sorry if you don't like dogs."

Laughing, I hug the little dog and beam. "I love dogs and who wouldn't adore this little angel?"

Sally grins. "She's no angel. We saw you coming, so I thought it best to let her get this out of her system outside. She can knock everything flying when she gets excited and I haven't had time to clear up today."

She beckons me inside and I carry Millie with me. As I look around, I laugh to myself. If Sally has cleared up in the last month, I'd be surprised. This place just appears even messier if that's possible.

Lowering Millie gently to the ground, she follows us into the bright kitchen wagging her tail. Sally reaches for the kettle and says politely, "Let me make you some tea, Rachel. I forgot to offer you some last time and felt bad."

Looking around hopefully for some sort of cake tin, I shake my head. "The cake was more than enough. Um… I was hoping I could maybe… um … buy some from you?"

Sally looks around in surprise. "You don't need to buy my cake. I'm sure I've got some around here if you want it."

She flicks on the kettle and then starts rummaging through a large larder in the corner of the kitchen. At one point I lose sight of her and just hear a triumphant, "Here it is. I knew I put one in here yesterday."

Proudly, she holds aloft a bright yellow cake tin and removes the lid, peering anxiously inside.

"Oh yes, I made this lemon cake. I put it in the yellow tin to remind me. Didn't work very well, did it?"

Fighting the urge to wrestle the tin from her in a very impolite manner, I just stare at the cake greedily. She reaches for a knife and cuts a huge slice and places it on a piece of kitchen paper saying apologetically, "Sorry, I've run out of plates. I decided to paint them yellow today and they're drying outside."

I don't think I even register that she spoke before I cram the cake into my mouth. It's like an explosion of everything good in life having a party in my mouth. Light, fluffy and full of taste. This woman is a genius.

She carries on making the tea and in between mouthfuls of cake, air needed to breathe and the manners I quickly remember I was brought up with, I say meaning every word, "You know, Sally, you should apply to be a contestant on The Great British Bake-off. I'm certain you'd win."

She looks confused. "What's that?"

Laughing, I realise Sally has never seen it. "It doesn't matter, it's just that this cake is exceptional."

She shrugs. "I've always loved to bake. Sometimes it's all I do."

She pushes over a mug of what looks like herbal tea and as I take it, I say with interest, "What else do you do? I mean, do you have a job?"

She nods. "I sell my Art online and locally."

I must look impressed because she says with excitement, "Come with me and I'll show you some."

I reluctantly leave the cake behind and follow her into a small room at the back of the cottage. This room is very different to the rest of the house. It's painted white and has bare boards that have no piles of clutter shielding it from view. Set in the middle is a large easel and around it is various paints and brushes. On the easel is a canvas that just has a few pencil lines sketching out an idea. However, the Art on the walls takes my breath away. Beautiful pictures of flowers, scenery, people, animals, you name it, she's captured it beautifully. I'm quite taken aback and just walk around studying them with wonder.

Sally, for all her quirks, is a true Artist in every way. These paintings come from the heart and spill out onto the canvas like precious jewels. I can almost reach out and pluck the flowers from the meadows. I fully expect the birds to sing in the sky before me and the tractors to move past as they plough the fields. The portraits of children should by rights be talking to me and telling me their names and the little painting I see of Bluebell cottage brings tears to my eyes.

Sally sees me reach out and touch it and smiles. "I did that for Molly. I'm going to visit her next week and thought I'd take her a piece of home along with her favourite cake."

I feel a lump form in my throat as I see the painting looking so beautiful and painted so lovingly. I say in a whisper, "She'll love this, Sally. That's such a beautiful thing to do."

She shrugs. "She was a good friend and I miss her."

Spinning around, I see the sadness in her eyes and say softly, "What brings you here, Sally? Have you always lived in the area?"

She shrugs. "I lived in Pembury for most of my life and hated it. I was always the odd one growing up. I never really fitted in and didn't have many friends. Nobody ever invited me to parties and didn't want me around. All I had was Art and so I studied it hard. I went to college and then rented this place as soon as I had the deposit. I make enough money selling my paintings to scrape by and what I can't pay for I pay in kind."

I say sadly, "Don't you get lonely?"

Sally shrugs. "Sometimes. I mean, I have friends who I see from time to time. Mainly Sheila and Bert, sometimes Jack and Max and a few of the locals but nobody I call a true friend as such."

"What about family? Do they live nearby?"

She nods. "Not far. I have a brother but he moved to Wales. Mum works as a nurse so doesn't have much time. My dad's a builder and works away a lot. I see them when I can but most of the time it's just me."

As we head back to the glorious cake, I say softly, "What about a boyfriend?"

She laughs and blushes a little. "No, I mean, have you looked at me, Rachel. I'm hardly the stuff of any man's dream. He'd have to be blind to want to date this."

She points to herself and I frown. "Don't sell yourself short, Sally. You're a beautiful woman and should be proud. Look at how clear your skin is and how beautiful your eyes are. So what if you dress differently? I'm guessing there's a man out there who would adore your style. You should have faith in yourself."

She shrugs. "I'm not bothered. I have Vixen and she doesn't judge. The boys that turned into men around here are still those childish kids I grew up with. They still remember the sad girl in the class who looked out of place and never really belonged. Anyway, I don't want a man to cloud my horizon. I just want a free view to keep my mind clear."

We sit sipping the strange tea and I try not to eye up the cake but obviously fail miserably because she smiles as she cuts me another slice. We hear the sound of a truck outside which draws our gaze to the window and I laugh when I see a brand-new bath tub sitting proudly on the back of a pickup. Jack comes out of Bluebell cottage and I'm ashamed to admit, I openly drool at the sight of them hauling that tub from the truck looking like man candy. Sally laughs softly. "Jack's a great guy."

Shaking myself back into the room, I say airily, "Yes, he seems nice. Have you known him long?"

She nods. "He's one of those kids I grew up with. He was never cruel like the rest though and more into sport than girls and yet one goes hand in hand with the other. The girls wanted to date him because he was good at it."

Feeling slightly light headed, I say, "It?"

She grins. "Sport. He was the best footballer, the best at basketball and could run a man down even from the back of the track. It's a powerful drug, success. The fact he has always been so good looking played a part and put the two together and bam."

I look out again and watch them disappear into the cottage. "So why hasn't he got a girlfriend now?"

She shakes her head. "He broke up with Fiona Styles two months ago. She had designs on them getting married and having babies. He wasn't fussed, so she went out one night and ended up going home with a friend of his. Needless to say, it ended. She only did it to make him jealous, but it backfired and she was history."

Trying not to appear too interested, I say lightly, "Do you think they'll get back together?"

"I doubt it. She joined an airline and moved near Gatwick, she's hardly here at all."

Her words remind me of our neighbour I've yet to meet and I say with interest, "I heard Max Summers is due back tomorrow. Do they work for the same airline?"

Sally laughs loudly. "I doubt it, that would be funny. You're in for a treat when Max arrives. Word of warning though, Rachel, don't pay any attention to him. He's got a wicked way with him that's just there for his own amusement. Take whatever he says with a pinch of salt and just enjoy his company. He's good for that at least."

I watch as Mack appears, closely followed by Jack and jump up feeling guilty.

"I'm sorry, Sally. I only came to buy some cake if I could and haven't even made them a cup of tea for their trouble; I should head back."

Sally nods and places the lid on the tin and offers it to me.

"Here, finish that one off with my compliments."

She could have given me a tin of gold and I wouldn't have been as grateful as I feel now.

I say with feeling, "Thank you so much. Let me repay the favour. Can I do something for you in return?"

She looks thoughtful. "You know, I wouldn't mind a hand clearing the front room tomorrow. I really should at least try and you would concentrate my mind rather than rushing off to paint."

Feeling happy that I can help, I nod, "I'd love to, shall we say 10am?"

She nods and I head towards the door, closely followed by Millie and Sally. Reaching down, I pat Millie on the head and smile my thanks.

"See you tomorrow, Sally, and thanks for the cake."

She nods and then closes the door quickly behind me. As I head back to Bluebell cottage clutching the treasure in my arms, I'm looking forward to tomorrow already.

♥11

Of all the men I've ever met in my sheltered life, Jack is the best company. When I return from Sally's, I make him a mug of tea and take him some of the gorgeous cake, although I do have to force myself to cut him a large slice.

I shamelessly hover in the doorway of the bathroom just so I can watch him work. What can I say, the sight of a man at work is a splendid thing and he is a fine example of one?

We spend a pleasant afternoon with me grilling him on every aspect of his life while skilfully dodging every question about mine.

It must be around 6 o'clock when he straightens up and says with satisfaction, "There, I think I'm done."

I look across at the bright shiny new bathtub, looking completely out of place in the shabby room. It shines like a spaceship that beamed in from planet luxury and the sight of the gleaming chrome almost makes me cry with happiness. How things have changed. I never cried over my old bathroom. In it - yes, but not tears of happiness.

Jack must see my expression because a soft look passes across his face and he says gently, "I'll turn on the water and you should be good to go."

Nodding, I look at him with gratitude. "I can't believe I feel so emotional over a bath. Thank you, Jack. I mean that from the bottom of my materialistic heart. I mean, who would want to wash in a bowl of water rather than a bath? Who would prefer to stand and feel the chill rather than relax in a bubble heaven while sipping a glass of wine, looking out to the moon? Who would rather hop on one leg while they try to reach every part of them, rather than allowing the hot, steamy, water, to infiltrate their whole body and wrap it in security and comfort?"

I notice Jack suddenly looks a little uncomfortable and realise I'm rambling – great, the crazy woman's back. So, I just shake my head and laugh self-consciously. "I'm sorry, you must think I'm strange."

He shakes his head and just for a second our eyes meet. The look in his makes my heart do an Irish jig and my head shout 'grab him, Rachel and never let him go. This man is too good to let escape.'

The silence hangs around us like a guest feeling they should leave. Time stands still and leans on the wall watching with interest. The birds outside hold their breath and the world stops spinning to take a look. This moment changes things between Jack and I and it's obvious neither one of us knows what to do next.

Jack recovers first and says awkwardly, "Um… well… I'm glad to be of help. Let me turn the water back on and test this baby out."

Shaking myself, I say hopefully, "What? You mean, like, have a bath."

He laughs, and the sound hits me in the part of me that likes to remain hidden. It wakes up and blinks a sleepy eye as it feels something long forgotten - interest.

He grins. "Well, if you insist, of course, you can but you'd probably rather test it out when you have your privacy."

He winks as I blush and try unsuccessfully to cover my embarrassment.

"Oh, of course, that's what I meant."

He heads out of the room to unblock the dam and restore comfort to my life and I look around me feeling slightly strange.

On the one hand, I can't wait to test this baby out. It's been a few days since I had the luxury of a bath and it's set me on edge mentally. Who knew the power of a bath tub? Then again, it means that Jack will leave and his reason for being here goes with him. That thought disturbs me and as he ventures back into the room, I try to rugby tackle my fickle heart to the ground and jump on it before it gets me into trouble again.

He grins. "Right let's test if this works."

He leans over the bath and turns on the taps and I try to look away from those capable hands that appear to be able to work magic. The water gushes out in short little bursts and he says with authority, "Just a little air, it will soon pull through."

What? I bring my mind back into the room from the place that desperate women go when faced with a desirable male, and watch as he fiddles with the shower attachment. When we see the water pour from the attachment like welcome rain in the desert, I almost cry with joy. I know it's only a shower but it's much more than that. It's one step forward in my new life. It's something positive in a dark time and the man who made it happen has restored my faith in men – a little.

As I watch Jack pack up his tools, I say nervously, "Listen, I should pay you for your trouble."

He shakes his head. "No need, I've been paid by the Steepleheads."

"I know, but even so, I feel bad. You've worked hard all day and haven't really stopped. Maybe you would like me to make you a meal to say thank you. Sort of payment in kind."

I blush as I say the words and he looks at me as if considering his options. He must be working out if I'm one of those desperate women who will do anything to play around with the hired help. I find myself holding my breath as I wait for his answer and manage to squeak. "Of course, that includes Millie, and um… maybe Sally as well if she wants."

I carry on at speed. "It's just that I don't have any friends here and it would be great to get to know you all."

Jack smiles gently and I watch in fascination as his eyes twinkle and makes a little piece of the ice in my heart melt.

"We would love to. I can't speak for Sally but Millie has never been known to turn down the offer of food. I'll head across and fetch them."

Watching him leave, I let out my breath and wonder what this feeling is inside me. It feels like relief, mixed in with a dash of hope and something else I can't quite place. Then panic joins the mix as I wonder what on earth a takeout queen, ready meal ranger and complete novice cook can possibly rustle up for the obvious gastronomic genius and man of many talents?

By the time I hear the scamper of tiny feet racing towards me, I've decided on a salad. You can't mess a salad up, surely, with some added crusty bread and cold meats. Throwing on some new potatoes, I'm pretty sure they cook themselves; I look up with the smug expression of the perfect housewife.

I am strangely pleased to see it's just Jack and Millie and hate myself for not wanting Sally here. Jack smiles as Millie jumps into my arms and proceeds to wash my face. "Sally's already eaten. She says thanks but she should really get on with her painting."

He laughs. "Millie obviously likes you. I'll take her if you're uncomfortable."

Snuggling into the little furry friend, I say gently, "Who couldn't love this? You're so lucky to have her, Jack. Maybe I should get a dog, after all, they are man's best friend so there's no reason why they can't be a woman's as well."

He laughs. "Spoken like a true feminist."

I grin. "What's wrong with that? I've always believed in doing anything I want to and see no boundaries. Don't get me wrong, I'm a bit of a dip in, dip out, sort of feminist because I also like to feel cared for and treated nicely. I don't hesitate to ask a man to do something he would obviously be better at than me."

He laughs. "So, you didn't wish you'd spent a lovely day installing the bath and shower yourself to prove you could?"

I shake my head. "No, it was much more fun watching you do it. What can I say, I'm a weak woman?"

Feeling slightly awkward again, as I stare into those woman baiting eyes, I lower Millie to the ground and set about washing my hands.

"Um… anyway, it's such a lovely evening, shall we eat outside?"

He nods, and we set about dishing up the quickest meal that I've ever made from scratch, without the need of a microwave, and proceed to take it outside.

I manage to find a bottle of wine and fill two glasses with some cold water to take away the thirst.

As we sit shoulder to shoulder on the rickety bench seat with the rusty iron table before me, I think I'm in paradise. The sun is losing its strength as it sucks the life out of the day and heads for pastures new. The birds sing for their supper and the temperature falls a little. All I can hear are the waves crashing on the beach below and the gentle sounds of nature complimenting it perfectly. As I sip my wine, with Jack pressed beside me and Millie with her head on his knee, I commit this moment to memory and file it away in the most treasured part of my soul. Does life really get any better than this?

♥12

Once again, the sun is shining as I wake and wonder if this place can get any better. I never used to take note of the weather but I'm becoming obsessed. Usually I shut myself away in my office from dark until dark. The only light I saw was through the glass but I was too busy to care. Thinking about my life, I wonder when things ceased to matter and were replaced by the desire to succeed and make money. Was I ever this girl who is revealing herself inside me? I never knew she was here but is someone I want to explore and work out if she is actually more important to me than the one I thought I was.

As I stretch my slumbered limbs, I relish the feel of contentment that washes over me like a familiar friend. This feeling is worth all the business deals in the world and worth more than the smart clothes and fancy apartment. This feeling is worth everything because it promises me something I've never had – freedom.

Humming to myself, I dress simply in a pale-yellow sundress in homage to Sally's love of yellow. Tying my hair in a messy ponytail, I leave the make up behind and head across the street to Sally's.

There is nobody to greet me as I cross the dusty road and no sounds of traffic or screaming sirens. Just the sunshine to keep me company and the birds to chat in my ear.

The door is open when I arrive, so I knock loudly and head inside.

"Sally, it's only Rachel come to help."

I hear a muffled, "I'm in the kitchen."

Stepping over the piles of dusty magazines and discarded paint palettes, I enter the kitchen with a smile that turns to one of amazement as I behold the sight before me.

Leaning back in the chair, with his legs up on the table, is a man. Not just any man either, a man that has that aura of knowing he's hot. A man that merely has to smirk in a woman's direction and she's running unashamedly after him. This man like all the others around here, is devastating.

He looks up with interest and grins wickedly. "Who do we have here then?"

Sally smiles. "Rachel's living in Molly's cottage. You know, I just told you about her."

I watch as he swings his feet from the table and stands. I swallow hard as he approaches, his eyes not breaking contact for a moment with mine and a sexy smile playing on his lips. His hair is cut close, and his eyes sparkle with mischief. Holding out his hand, he takes mine, and it feels like a sexual act as he caresses it with his thumb and squeezes it lightly before saying huskily, "I'm Max, pleased to meet you."

I reply but my voice comes out like an opera singer as I say. "Um... hi, Max. I'm Rachel, pleased to meet you."

Forgetting to drop my hand, he pulls me with him to the table and then gallantly holds out a chair, saying, "Allow me."

I sit as if on autopilot and Sally smiles. "Morning, Rachel. Max just dropped in, he arrived last night. He lives in Bayside Manor at the top of the hill."

I nod as if I've lost the power to speak as Max resumes his seat and leans in to look at me. "So, Rachel. I must say, you're a sight for sore eyes. Aside from Sally here, this place is extremely lacking in hot female company."

Sally rolls her eyes and grins and I stare at her. I mean, really stare. Goodness, Sally suddenly looks years younger. Her eyes are sparkling and her cheeks tinged pink with excitement. She holds herself straight and runs her fingers through her hair self-consciously. The look she is giving Max is one of total adoration. Not the type where a woman wants a man. The type of look that speaks of a deep-rooted friendship and a love of one person to another that transcends mere infatuation. Max looks at Sally with the same look and my heart sings. This is pure friendship if ever I saw it. They are obviously happy to be together and once again, I think on my life and can't ever remember somebody looking at me like that.

Max laughs as Sally pushes a cup of her strange tea towards him.

"Thanks, babe. You know, try as I might, I can never find the like of this tea anywhere else."

He winks at me as he sips it and I stifle a grin as Sally rolls her eyes. "I'm guessing you never tried. I know you, prefer coffee in its darkest form and I bet you only drink tea here because it's the only thing on offer."

He nods. "You know me so well, Sally. I only come home to sample your culinary delights, anyway. So, babe, do I have to beg, or are you going to give me what I want?"

Sally laughs softly as she reaches down and plucks yet another cake tin from god only knows where. "Here you go, I made this one just the way you like it."

I wonder if it would be rude of me to snatch that tin from his hands and run? He must see the greed in my eyes because he laughs softly and stands quickly. "Ok, ladies. As much as I would love to stay and get acquainted with our hot new friend, I need to get back."

As he stands, I notice he's dressed in joggers and a tight-fitting vest top. He has trainers on his feet and as I allow my gaze to linger on his impressive biceps, he catches my eye and smirks. "I'll leave you both with an invitation to party at mine tonight. It will be good to catch up, shall we say 7.30? Sally, no need to bring anything, the cake was payment enough. Rachel, bring yourself and the desire to party hard and I'll provide the means."

He winks as he passes and leans down, whispering, "I insist."

Then he says cheekily, "I'll see myself out ladies, have a good day."

When he leaves, the air comes back into the room and I pounce on it eagerly. Taking a few deep breaths, I try to get my heart rate back to normal. Sally watches the way he went and laughs softly.

"That was Max. He's quite a character, isn't he?"

I just nod as she carries on, apparently now in her own little world.

"He's such a cad though. He loves the affect he has on women and plays it to his advantage all the time. The women around here tick the dates off their calendar until they reach the large red circle of his arrival."

I laugh and roll my eyes. "He's a player then?"

Sally laughs. "A total man whore and lover of all things female. You won't be safe from him until he heads off into the sunset. He always does you know because his time is limited."

I nod. "I heard he was a pilot; he must be extremely busy."

Sally nods. "Yes, he's always away but makes time to check on this place."

I can't stop myself and say nonchalantly, "Does he have a girlfriend? I mean, surely there must have been one."

Sally shakes her head. "No, he's never brought a girl home. The only people who use this house are his close family. I know they're coming for the summer, so he's probably making sure everything's in place."

She jumps up. "Anyway, we had better get started otherwise the light will go and I have some painting to do this afternoon."

As she hands me a bucket filled with all manner of untouched cleaning products, she says shyly, "You really don't have to do this you know. I would give you the cake gladly. I don't expect anything in return."

I quickly grab the bucket and frown, "You don't get out of it that easily, Sally. Show me where you want me to start."

I follow her into the front room and look around in amazement. This place must surely be a fire hazard and be home to many unsavoury insects and I almost faint with fear as I see a large spider eyeing me up from the corner of the room.

Sally sighs. "I'm not sure how it got so bad. I don't come in here much, probably because it's so messy. I spend most of my time in the art room and kitchen."

Thinking of her messy kitchen, I smile to myself. Sally obviously just has the need to create, not clean. I feel happy that I can help her even in this small way.

As we start sorting through her things, I steel myself for the task ahead.

As we work, we talk and I discover Sally is much more interesting than I first thought. She's witty and good company and I soon know everything there is to know about the people in Perivale. After a while, the floor starts to clear, revealing a pleasant room that looks over the street outside. The garden before it is pretty, with a few flowering shrubs and ornamental weeds. As I clean the grime from the windows, I relish the sunlight hitting the far corners of the room. Looking across at Sally who has been distracted by a magazine, I say firmly, "Help me get these curtains down. I'll give them a wash and then I can get to every corner of this window and frame."

She looks up guiltily and heads across to help. As I balance on the edge of a chair, I say breathlessly, "You know, I could always help out. I'm happy to come here and tidy up a few days a week so you can concentrate on painting. I don't have anything else to do and would love to help."

Sally's eyes shine and she looks so touched it melts my heart. "Would you really want to, Rachel? I mean, you don't have to do that."

I smile. "I would love to. It's good to have a little company, anyway. I don't have much of that and obviously there's a tempting reason why I'm offering."

She laughs. "Cake."

I nod. "Yes, cake."

She smiles and I say thoughtfully, "You know, you really do have a talent and not just for painting. Have you ever tried supplying Mulligans in town? I'm betting there's a few places around here who would pay good money for a supply of your cake."

Sally laughs loudly. "I'm not interested in making money from baking, Rachel. I do it because I love it. If I had to bake it would put pressure on me and then I'd end up hating it. No, painting makes me money and far more than selling a few cakes would."

Immediately, I'm curious and say airily, "So how much would you charge say for that painting you did of Bluebell cottage?"

She shrugs. "House portraits are around £1500 depending on their size and detail. Family portraits are around £5-6000 depending on how many members."

I almost fall off my chair and stare at her incredulously. "That's amazing, Sally. I never knew. Do you get many commissions?"

She nods and reaches behind her where a large notebook sits with a mug on top of it. As she flicks through it I see rows and rows of entries and she sighs. "I currently have 20 orders and a few quotes waiting. I'm not sure when I'll get them done."

Thank goodness there's a chair handy because I need it to sit down heavily on. "That's some business you've got there."

Shrugging, she picks up the feather duster and studies it by holding it to the light and spinning it around. "Isn't this pretty, Rachel? Look at the shapes the feathers make against the sunlight."

Laughing to myself, I smile at her fondly. "Good for Sally. She's doing something she loves and the money is unimportant at the end of the day. She frowns as she replaces the duster and looks around. "It's why this place never sees this duster. I just don't have time."

"Then why don't you employ a cleaner?"

She laughs. "That would be silly, Rachel. Why would I pay someone to do something I could do myself?"

"Because you aren't doing it and would be happier to paint than clean, so you would be helping out another person by employing them to do a job you hate."

She looks unconvinced so I say, "Like Jack. You dog sit and he does the garden and odd jobs in return. It's no different paying money than favours, especially if you have it."

Sally shakes her head. "I don't want people in here, Rachel. They judge and they talk. I've been the subject of a lot of gossip over the years and none of it good. It's best like this. I have a few friends and Vixen and that's all I want. I like my life just the way it is."

As she speaks, I am starting to realise an important lesson. Not everyone places the same value on things others take for granted. I shouldn't make her feel bad for not wanting to follow the usual path. If anything, she should be applauded for sticking to her guns. Maybe I can learn a thing or two from Sally and so I smile. "That's fine. You live life just the way you want to and don't let anyone tell you otherwise."

We carry on working until the room is tidy and look with satisfaction at the neat piles of objects waiting for a home. There is a charity shop pile, refuse pile and pile of memories to file away. The room looks clean and inviting and the windows sparkle catching the sun's rays and the furniture groans with relief at being free from the clutter. Sally looks around with amazement. "You know, I forgot I had half of this furniture. You're a miracle worker, Rachel."

I shake my head. "Not really. I just have a little time and nothing to do. Like I said, I'm happy to help."

Sally grins "Then let me pay you what you earned. I have a cake kicking around somewhere that needs a home."

Feeling suddenly elated, I follow her hungrily from the room.

♥13

As I get ready for the party this evening, I wonder what on earth is happening here. Just a few short days ago I was a busy business woman with no time to even paint her nails and definitely no inclination. Yet, here I am now, sifting through my small wardrobe of choice, wondering what just happened? Can life really be one thing and then change so dramatically? When I came here, it was with the sole intention of hiding from the world. I never expected to meet anyone; let alone the lovely people I have.

Then there's my heart. Nervously I take a look inside at something I have wrapped in cotton wool and locked away to heal. Daring to think about Spencer and Camilla, I am surprised to find the ache has eased slightly, and no longer makes me feel as sick as it did. Testing the water, a little more, I think about Perivale and what this now means to me. I feel my heart lift a little as it's filled with warm sunshine and happiness. Maybe this is where my heart belongs. It certainly feels like that but how can it after such a short period?

Then my heart starts beating just a little faster as I think of Logan and his angry, impatient, stare. That brooding look that somehow makes me go weak at the knees and fires up something in my soul. I'm not sure what that feeling is yet. It's probably best he went away giving me some time to settle down, away from his complicated company.

My thoughts turn to Jack and that feeling of confusion softens, and a lightness fills my heart. I find myself smiling as I picture his gentle look and familiar stare. Why does Jack make me feel settled and as if I'm home?

Somehow Max barges his way past my thoughts of Jack and fills my head with his cocky smirk and wicked eyes. That man is trouble and I feel a shiver of excitement as I think of the evening ahead. What is it about this man that has made me react so strongly after just a brief meeting? I meet lots of guys every day at work but none have caused this explosion of feelings in me.

I see many an interested look thrown my way from across a boardroom table. Many looks as I rush from one tube station to another and many smiles and nods of intent as I head out for drinks at night. Not one of them held my attention like these three have.

Then there's my fiancé. The man I'm supposed to love and engaged to marry in just six months from now. My family adore him - I think, and so do I. Or do I? I've barely thrown a thought in his direction since I got here. I have no desire to take the 'do not disturb' from my phone and call him just to hear his voice. It doesn't bother me if I think of him worrying about where I've gone and I don't miss feeling his arms wrapped around me as we sleep at night.

Throwing a look at my phone, I wonder what notifications it's hiding. Angry messages will turn to pleading ones to ones of panic. I expect there are several voice messages and emails each one angrier than the last. The meetings I had set up would have been hastily rearranged and I expect my family are worried about me.

Thinking about them, I feel a little bad. The voice message I left my father seems a little lacking as I think how worried he must be. You see, this isn't me. This person who took off at a moment's notice and left everything behind. This isn't Rachel Asquith, who plans every detail in triplicate and allows others to dictate her every move. When did the girl I was become this woman? It was so gradual I never realised I had lost the most important I owned. My freedom.

Sighing, I file that thought away for another day and look at my totally unsuitable choice of clothes. I didn't pack any party wear so decide on a black top with matching black jeans. I grab a white cardigan and then brush my hair until it dances around my shoulders. A minimal amount of make-up completes the look with a splash of my favourite scent. Slipping on some ballerina pumps I stare at myself critically. Hardly smart or designed to attract. Perfect, because the less encouragement I give anyone the better. I'm not here to find a man,

I'm here to find a woman – me. I must take a leaf out of Sally's book and shut the world away for a little and just accept the friendship on offer until I work out what I'm doing.

A loud knock on the door brings me back to the present, and I feel surprised. Maybe it's Sally. A little early but as she doesn't track time, it's the most likely explanation.

However, as I fling the door open my traitorous heart beats a little faster and a smile springs to my lips as I see an extremely desirable male filling the doorway and grinning sexily.

"Evening, Rachel, how's the shower?"

"Like a little piece of heaven. I can't thank you enough."

Jack laughs and says lightly. "I thought I'd walk you and Sally to Max's. He told me he'd asked you both over and I thought you may need the protection."

Laughing, I beckon him in.

"I think you're right. Come in and I'll fix you a drink. I told Sally I'd meet her at 7.15. We still have time for some Dutch courage before then."

Jack follows me into the kitchen and I reach for two glasses and the bottle of wine in the fridge.

"Would you like wine? I'm afraid I don't have any beers."

Jack nods. "Wine would be good."

I busy myself pouring the drinks and try to ignore the fact I'm happy to see him.

He takes the glass from my hand and I say lightly, "Shall we take it outside? It's such a lovely evening and I can't get used to having a garden. I only have a balcony in London and this is a luxury I never knew I was missing."

He follows me to the little rusty bench and we sit looking out across the bay. The sun is getting ready to brighten another continent, and the moon is making us think of calling it a day. It's like the changing of the guard as they take their rightful places as governed by nature. It feels a little like that now as Jack sits beside me and laughs gently.

"What did you make of Max?"

Taking a sip of wine, I smile. "I'm not sure. It was a quick meeting but I could tell he was a character."

Jack laughs. "You could say that."

"How do you know him?"

"He's a friend of mine from way back. We went to school together and were quite a team."

Smiling, I can just picture it. Two drop dead gorgeous guys unleashed on the girls of the neighbourhood. I'm guessing they were indeed quite a team.

He carries on. "Max didn't want to stay around long though. He was one of those guys who had it all. Good looks, a fantastic personality and clever too. As soon as he could he was off to university and that was that. He bought Bayside Manor when it came up for auction. His grandmother died and left a small fortune. He inherited half and his brother the other half. We all expected Max to buy a house near his work but he surprised us all and bought that. It shows you can never really escape this place. His family moved away years ago but they like to come back for the summer. They spend at least four weeks here in the summer and usually head back for Christmas."

I picture Max's family and compare them to mine and say out loud. "It must be nice to have a close family."

Jack says gently. "It is."

Turning to look at him, I see all the riches of the world in his eyes. He seems happy and settled and obviously content. There is no weariness and strain showing of someone who doubts who they are. Jack appears to have everything.

I say softly. "Tell me about your family, Jack."

He smiles and I can I've touched on a subject close to his heart. He says happily. "My parents still live in Pembury but my sister moved away. She works in Bristol and lives with her boyfriend. They visit when they can but it's not the same. I've never wanted to leave but recognise the need in others. Pembury is a small fish in a very large exciting sea.

Not many stay to call it home but I wouldn't want it any other way."

As I watch the sun lose its heat and turn orange as it makes its journey south, I think about what it must have been like growing up here. It's the kind of place I read about in the books I devoured as a child. Nothing bad happened in places like this and everything was perfect. As I grew up my tastes changed and the books I read spoke of darker times and conflict. Excitement that surpassed the need for comfort and familiarity. Maybe that's what makes people spread their wings and take flight from the safety of home. Seeking out adventure and excitement and something they crave more than this. The unknown.

Jack nudges me and smiles. "Come on, Sally will be waiting and we need to save Max from drinking the place dry before we've even got started. Prepare yourself, Rachel. This evening will be stranger than most."

♥14

We collect Sally on the way and I laugh as I see what she's wearing. She is the lady in red. Bright red hair, red jumpsuit covered in white flowers and red lace-up boots. Jack laughs and says cheekily, "Wow, Sally. When you go for a theme you go all out."

She grins as she locks the door of her little cottage. "Well, if something's worth doing, it's worth doing well."

Jack eyes up a large bag she's carrying hopefully. "I don't suppose there's a cake in there by any chance?"

She nods. "Red velvet."

We laugh and Jack reaches out to take the bag from her. "Then allow me to help you with it."

She frowns. "Ok, but no shaking it around. I want it intact by the time we get there."

We head up the hill towards Bayside manor and I wonder what this evening will be like. Sally and Jack chatter away like old friends and I can tell this is a journey they have taken many times.

As we near our destination, I look with wonder at the magnificent building that appears to dominate the skyline. Bayside manor is impressive and sits like the brightest Jewel on top of the most valuable crown as its windows sparkle in the last rays of the diminishing sunlight.

We walk through two impressive stone columns that hold in place a large metal gate. The driveway is stunning and flanked by various shrubs and statues. It's certainly steep and I feel a little out of breath as I make the climb.

Once we reach the house, I take a deep breath and look around me in awe, saying, "Wow, I feel as if I'm on top of the world up here."

Sally nods. "Impressive, isn't it? You can see for miles and I'm sure there isn't a more magnificent view than this in the whole world."

Jack nods. "I agree. Max certainly knew what he was doing when he bought this place. This view will never get old."

Then we hear a loud, "What are you doing hanging around here, guys? The party's inside."

Spinning around, my breath catches as I see Max leaning against the wall looking freshly showered and extremely hot. He has changed into a tight-fitting t-shirt with the words 'Come and get it' emblazoned across his chest. He's wearing cargo shorts and flip flops and his hair, although cut short, is spiked with gel at the front. He has this assured air that he wears well and appears confident and relaxed as he winks at Sally and says with affection. "Babe, what a picture you look. You know red's my favourite colour and you, of course, are my favourite girl."

I watch as he opens his arms and Sally moves into them. His arms fold around her and he squeezes her hard saying softly, "I've missed you, babe."

He looks up and sees Jack and grins. I sense the brotherly love and friendship between them as Max says, "Jack. Good to see you, bro."

Jack moves across and joins their little circle. Max pulls him into the hug and for some reason it brings a tear to my eye. These three have a friendship that can't be bought. It's built up over many years and grown into something beautiful. This is a strong bond of something so rare I feel the poorer because I have no such thing in my life. I stand watching feeling a little awkward until Max looks across and smiles sweetly. "Come over here, girl. Don't just stand there, you don't escape this little love fest you know."

It feels a little weird but I do as he asks. Jack pulls me into the group and we stand there hugging weirdly as Max says happily. "I've missed you guys. I'm happy that three have become four though, it balances our group out nicely, don't you think?"

Sally and Jack laugh as I blush redder than Sally's suit as they all look at me.

Jack smiles and squeezes my shoulder and Sally gives my waist a little tug as she says warmly,

"Well, I'm glad Rachel's here. She can help me keep you guys in check because I'm struggling to do it on my own."

Max winks and drops a light kiss on her head as a car can be heard approaching. We pull apart and Max grins. "Here they come, late as always."

We all stand to the side as a car screeches to a standstill and I smile as Bert and Sheila join us. Bert grumbles, "Sorry we're late. Sheila was faffing around as usual and I told her a million times to get a move on but would she listen?"

Sheila says loudly, "Oh, for god's sake, Bert. You had that car revving up outside at least 30 minutes before we were due to go. You always do, you know. It drives me mad. I only need to suggest going somewhere and there he is, sitting in the damn car, tapping the steering wheel and honking his horn. Anyone would think you have nothing better to do."

Bert grins. "I don't. It's called retirement."

Sheila shrieks. "So, the list of jobs I gave you is nothing to do, is it? Last time I checked they were still waiting. You know, Bert Richardson, you've always been the same. If you can get out of doing any jobs around the house, you will. That skirting board is still hanging off in the hallway and that picture I bought at the village hall sale is still gathering dust on the top of the wardrobe. Maybe a bit of time management would be a good thing instead of hassling me with your car."

Max laughs. "Sheila, babe, I need a woman like you in my life. The trouble is, Bert already stole you away and nobody will ever measure up."

Sheila huffs but I see her eyes sparkle. "Keep your smooth talking for someone who wants it, Maxwell. I'm just here for the alcohol."

Max laughs. "Then follow me and I'll ply you with it. Who knows, babe, I may get lucky and you'll realise I'm the man you dream of at night and old Bert here will be history."

Bert says loudly, "I think that's my dream you're talking about. Just think, peaceful solitude to watch the birds all day. No nagging and I could eat what I want and watch what I want. I hope there's a lot of alcohol in this place because you've raised my hopes now, son."

Sheila rolls her eyes as Max laughs. "Don't give me that bird watching rubbish, Bert. We all know your binoculars are always trained on a different kind of bird down at the beach."

Bert winks. "I told you that in confidence."

They head inside arguing as they go and Sally follows them chatting to Max. Jack rolls his eyes. "They're all mad."

I fall into step beside him and say wistfully. "Nice mad though. You all seem so happy and comfortable with each other. Is this usual, I mean, do you often get together like this?"

Jack nods. "It's tradition. Whenever Max returns, we always spend the first night with him. A sort of catch up which settles him in. He likes to hear the local gossip and reconnect with the place. Max may have the largest house in the area but he hates being on his own. We try to fill this house with laughter and friendship because it makes him feel at home."

We step inside the huge doors and I look around with interest. We are standing in a large panelled hall with a beautiful parquet floor that's polished to perfection. Huge flower arrangements fill the air with their amazing scent and sit proudly on console tables that sparkle with cleanliness.

I say with surprise. "My goodness, this place is spotless. Does Max have OCD or something?"

Jack laughs. "No, a housekeeper called Mrs Abrahams who's like a sergeant major. She keeps this place immaculate and Max absolutely adores her."

I look around with interest. "Is she here?"

Jack laughs. "Probably as far away as possible. She wouldn't be able to watch as Max systematically takes apart all her hard work. You see, Max may be extremely tidy and meticulous with everything in his working life, but he's a total slob in his private one. It would make Mrs Abrahams weep if she saw how he treats this place and I expect she does when he's left. It probably takes her weeks to right the place but she'll always forgive him because that's who Max is. A lovable rogue who somehow manages to make everyone love him."

We reach a large room that is impressive but cosy at the same time. Huge comfortable settees are placed around an open fire that is home to yet another flower arrangement. The furniture in the room is strangely modern in contrast to its surroundings. Max is standing by a set of open patio doors with a panoramic view of the bay and pours us some drinks. "Help yourself, guys, we need to toast my return like the hero I am."

We all grab a glass of champagne and he holds his up and says loudly, "To friends old and new and a couple of crazy weeks ahead."

We all repeat the words and as I feel the cool liquid slip down my throat and dance happily inside me, I feel a happiness I rarely feel. This place - these people, are magical and fate has played a trump card in bringing me here.

We all take our seats and I listen to the group talking about people and places they share a familiarity with. Max looks interested as they fill him in on the local gossip and Jack leans across and whispers, "This must be boring for you, Rachel."

I shake my head vigorously. "Not at all. It's quite interesting, really."

Max looks across and says loudly, "Hey, Jack, swap seats. I want to talk to Rachel. You can talk to her when I've gone."

Jack smiles apologetically before heading to talk to Sheila and Max flops down beside me and smiles cheekily. "So, Rachel. Our newest member and yet the most interesting."

Looking across at Sally talking with animation to Bert, I laugh. "I doubt that very much. Sally is definitely the most interesting person I've ever met."

I watch Max's eyes soften as he looks across at her and says softly, "You know, Sally is my sister from another mother. I love that girl with everything I've got. She's such a lovely person and I just wish she'd stop hiding away in that dusty cottage and go out there and conquer the world."

I nod. "She's very talented but also happy in what she does. She told me she hides away from the world and I'm guessing it's because she's been betrayed by it."

Max nods bitterly. "She's always been considered strange and weird. People call her eccentric as if it's a bad thing and wrote her off years ago. She keeps herself to herself and only lets a select few in. The sad thing is, behind all that madness is a heart that beats larger than most. She's funny, witty and wise and yet won't allow anyone close enough to see it. I wish she would let me show her off to the world but she won't hear of it."

We watch Sally laugh loudly at something Bert says and I watch a small smile twitch on Max's lips. His eyes soften and yet I also see a sadness in them that makes my breath hitch. Then, just as quickly as it comes, it goes, and he smiles sweetly. "So, tell me, Rachel, what brings you here?"

I shrug sadly. "A cheating fiancé and a dissatisfaction with how my life is heading. I wanted to get away to re-evaluate what I want in life."

Max looks interested. "Now that's a story worth listening to."

Laughing, I shake my head. "Not really. I'd rather hear about your life. I hear you're a pilot, what airline do you work for?"

Max looks surprised and his eyes crinkle up at the edges as he laughs softly. The room has suddenly gone quiet and Sheila says in astonishment. "What, you don't know what Max does, Rachel?"

I feel a little awkward as they all look at me incredulously. "Um... I was told he's a pilot, why, is that wrong?"

Jack grins and rolls his eyes as Max say proudly, "I am but the planes I fly take no passengers."

The others all look amused and Sally says, "That's why I'm wearing red tonight, to make Max feel at home."

I shake my head, "Sorry, I'm still confused."

Max grins. "I fly Jets, Rachel. I'm no civilian pilot, I'm a member of the RAF."

I'm impressed. "That's amazing. How long have you been in the Airforce?"

He shrugs. "Too long."

Sheila chips in. "Tell her the whole story, Max."

He laughs and winks before adding, "I'm currently flying in the Red Arrows. You know, the RAF display team. You're looking at Red 4, we practice hard and attend every event going. We fly all over the world in formation and perform perilous tricks just for the public's pleasure."

I can't believe it and say excitedly, "That's amazing. I've seen them on the TV but never in person. You must be very good at flying."

Jack groans. "Don't make his head bigger than it already is, Rachel. Max may be some super pilot but he's still an annoying one."

Max throws a cushion at Jack's head and says loudly, "You're just jealous because I'm a star and you wish you were me."

Jack throws the cushion back and soon they are rolling around the floor, play fighting like two little boys. Sheila bellows, "Stop fighting, boys. Whatever will Rachel think of us."

She looks across. "I'm sorry, Rachel. These two are always like this. They never really grew up and are always arguing."

Sally grins as Bert says, "You know, I always fancied joining the army. Lots of foreign travel and the chance to wear a uniform and attract the girls."

Sheila snorts. "Lots of foreign travel. One - you're the sort who thinks a day out in Pembury is exotic. Two - you hate foreign food as you call it. I mean, even a barbeque is out of bounds in your book. Three - you're afraid of flying and four - you get palpitations if a woman so much as asks you the time. Honestly Bert, you do say the strangest things some time."

Max jumps up. "Speaking of barbeques, I've got one on the go outside."

He looks at Bert. "Don't worry, I've got a large, juicy, steak with your name on it with absolutely no foreign spices on it. Just as you like it."

Bert grins. "Now you come to mention it, I am feeling rather hungry."

We follow Max outside and I stare in amazement. The view from up here is mind blowing. Sally stands beside me and says wistfully, "Impressive isn't it? I love this place so much and come here often. Max lets me come here whenever I want for inspiration. I actually can't count how many paintings I've done of that view and yet they're all different."

I nod. "I can believe that. You know, Sally, Max seems a great guy. He obviously thinks the world of you too."

Sally smiles softly. "He's great, isn't he?"

I feel curious and whisper, "Have you ever... um... been tempted to ... um..."

Sally nudges me. "No, I have not. I know what you're getting at and that would be like incest in my book. No, Max is like an older brother to me, much like Jack. They are always there but I never think of them in that way."

"Has there ever been anyone special in your life, Sally?"

She sighs. "Not really. I've sort of given up on romance. I think that's for other people, Rachel. In case you've missed it, I'm a little strange. I think I've lived on my own for so long it would be strange having anyone invade my space."

I shrug. "How do you know until you've tried it? I'm guessing there's someone out there for you just itching to try and make you happy."

Sally laughs. "Then he'd be a fool. I mean, he'd have to be to sign up to my life. No, I'm just happy with Vixen and my Art. I mean, what can possibly compare to that? Not everybody wants a man. Some people's fairy tales don't involve romance. My particular one is painting something better than I have ever done before. Discovering a new flavour that makes my taste buds dance and hearing the contented purr of my furry friend as she sits on my lap at night watching the sun go down. That's the fairy tale in my life. I have good friends who I adore and a lovely cottage I abuse terribly. A man would be like a dark cloud overshadowing everything else I hold dear. I'm not ready to let the darkness in, and probably never will be."

She smiles as Max calls her and leaves me wondering if she's a genius. Sally's right, we don't need a partner to define us as a person. We need to feel comfortable with ourselves above everything else. I suppose we are born on our own and owe it to do right by ourselves first. People may come and go in our lives but the only one with you to the end is yourself. That's the person you nurture. The person you do the right thing for and the person you protect with everything you've got. Sally's right but wrong about the most important thing. You owe it to yourself to let love into your life. Nothing compares to sharing your life with someone who completes your soul. It's just not that easy to find them.

"Penny for them."

I blink away my rambling thoughts and focus on one man who appears to come close. Jack holds out a plate of food and says sweetly, "I took the liberty of grabbing a mixture of things. You looked a little lost, so I did the honours."

Smiling gratefully, I take the plate and sit down on the grass overlooking the bay. Jack flops beside me and smiles gently. "You know, I'm glad you moved here."

I look at him with surprise. "Why?"

His eyes twinkle softly and hold my attention. "Because you look as if you need this place to set you on the right path. I can tell you have a lot to think of and can't think of a better place to do it."

As I take a bite of food, I nod in agreement. "You know, this place feels more like home to me than my own. Does that sound weird?"

He laughs softly. "Not at all. I couldn't imagine being anywhere else in the world. This place is special, the people in it, the surrounding area and the fact it stays constant in a changing world. Some say it's dull but it will always be paradise to me."

As we sit side by side on the top of the world, I must agree with him. This place certainly is paradise.

By the time the darkness falls we are all merry and getting increasingly louder. All of my inhibitions disappeared along with the sunshine and the drinks just keep on coming.

particular one is painting something better than I have ever done before. Discovering a new flavour that makes my taste buds dance and hearing the contented purr of my furry friend as she sits on my lap at night watching the sun go down. That's the fairy tale in my life. I have good friends who I adore and a lovely cottage I abuse terribly. A man would be like a dark cloud overshadowing everything else I hold dear. I'm not ready to let the darkness in, and probably never will be."

She smiles as Max calls her and leaves me wondering if she's a genius. Sally's right, we don't need a partner to define us as a person. We need to feel comfortable with ourselves above everything else. I suppose we are born on our own and owe it to do right by ourselves first. People may come and go in our lives but the only one with you to the end is yourself. That's the person you nurture. The person you do the right thing for and the person you protect with everything you've got. Sally's right but wrong about the most important thing. You owe it to yourself to let love into your life. Nothing compares to sharing your life with someone who completes your soul. It's just not that easy to find them.

"Penny for them."

I blink away my rambling thoughts and focus on one man who appears to come close. Jack holds out a plate of food and says sweetly, "I took the liberty of grabbing a mixture of things. You looked a little lost, so I did the honours."

Smiling gratefully, I take the plate and sit down on the grass overlooking the bay. Jack flops beside me and smiles gently. "You know, I'm glad you moved here."

I look at him with surprise. "Why?"

His eyes twinkle softly and hold my attention. "Because you look as if you need this place to set you on the right path. I can tell you have a lot to think of and can't think of a better place to do it."

As I take a bite of food, I nod in agreement. "You know, this place feels more like home to me than my own. Does that sound weird?"

He laughs softly. "Not at all. I couldn't imagine being anywhere else in the world. This place is special, the people in it, the surrounding area and the fact it stays constant in a changing world. Some say it's dull but it will always be paradise to me."

As we sit side by side on the top of the world, I must agree with him. This place certainly is paradise.

By the time the darkness falls we are all merry and getting increasingly louder. All of my inhibitions disappeared along with the sunshine and the drinks just keep on coming.

Max is good company and as we sit slouching on his settees, he shouts, "Ok everyone. Let's all share our porn names."

Sally giggles as Sheila looks horrified. "Good god, Max. What on earth are you talking about?"

Max grins. "It's simple. You take the name of your first pet and your mother's maiden name. For instance, my porn name is, Wiggles Wood. Wiggles was my rabbit and Wood my mother's maiden name."

He turns to Jack. "Your turn."

Jack grins. "Wolfie Wilde."

We all laugh and Max says loudly, "Not your real porn name you sex beast."

Jack winks as Sheila looks excited. "Goodness, Jack, they say the quiet ones are the worst."

She giggles, "Ok, mine is, Muffy Monroe."

I can feel myself shaking as the noise erupts in the room. Bert shakes his head. "Who was Muffy?"

She smiles fondly, "My hamster. Sweet little girl she was. Spent her whole life running around a big wheel in circles. Funny how my life turned out the same."

Bert rolls his eyes and says cheekily, "I was Jonathan Richardson."

Sheila says loudly, "Good god, Bert, didn't you have any friends? I mean, fancy calling a pet, Jonathan."

Jack laughs. "I can just see you now, Bert. When your school pals asked what you did at the weekend." He mimics. "Oh, Jonathan and I went swimming or Jonathan and I went on an adventure in the woods."

Max laughs. "Not very porn like, is it? Sheila, you're winning so far, babe. I would love to meet Muffy Monroe on a dark night."

Sheila winks as Sally says with a laugh, "Mine was Estelle Rogers."

We all laugh as Jack says, "What on earth was Estelle?"

She grins. "A Guinea pig. She was particularly fancy and had this amazing plume on her back. I thought she looked like a film star so wanted to call her something exotic."

They turn to me and I roll my eyes. "Ok, mine was Dottie Sinclair. Not half as good as some of these. I think Sheila has this one in the bag."

Sally says with interest, "Who was Dottie?"

I smile, thinking of my faithful friend. "A black Labrador. She was gorgeous and lived until she was 12. I felt as if my world ended when she died."

Sally nods. "I can imagine. They become part of the family, don't they?"

We fall silent as we think of our pets and then Max booms, "Come on porn stars, fill your glasses and I'll put on a movie. Anyone for Top Gun?"

We laugh as Max fills our glasses and then we settle down to watch a movie, none of us in any hurry to end this night and just happy to chill with good company and alcohol.

It must be around 2am when the night draws to a natural close. Due to the large amount of alcohol we've consumed, Max insists we all stay and shows us to beautifully made up rooms. Bert and Sheila are the first to retire and wave us goodnight. After a while, I feel my eyes closing and Jack whispers, "You should grab some sleep, Rachel. I'll walk with you because I've had enough."

I smile gratefully and say goodnight to Max and Sally, who are sitting together on the largest couch. Max has his back to the arm and is laying with his legs out. Sally is leaning back on him with his arms wrapped around her as they watch the end of yet another movie. They smile sweetly as we head off and I whisper to Jack, "I wish they were a couple. They look good together."

Jack laughs softly. "They love each other too much to risk it."

I look at him in surprise. "What do you mean?"

"It means that there are many types of love. The love of your pet or your family or the love of a fantastic view or a place you hold dear. Then there's the love of a fine wine and amazing food; the love between lovers or that of friends. The love they have – we have, is special because nothing will ever get in its way. That love is the hardest to find because it's the most precious. Why would they take a chance on spoiling something so amazing?"

We reach a door at the end of the hallway and Jack smiles sweetly. "So, here we are. You're in here and I'm across the hall. You're perfectly safe here, Rachel so make sure you get some sleep. Thanks for a great evening and I'll see you for breakfast, although knowing Max it will probably be brunch by the time he surfaces."

Just for a second, we share a look. Something happens that makes me question everything. It's the feeling growing inside me that I don't want to go anywhere. I don't want to leave this place, these people and strangely most of all, Jack. His expression tells me he feels something too and I hold my breath and wonder if fate has a few more tricks up her sleeve. Then he smiles and says softly, "Good night, Rachel."

Thankfully the bed I sleep in does its job well. Despite all the questions running around my head, my body succumbs to the comfort and drifts into a deep sleep. There are no decisions to be made in my dreams. In fact, there are no dreams. Just pure, blissful sleep, which I need more than anything at this moment in time.

♥15

It takes me a moment to remember where I am when I wake the following morning. The day started hours ago it seems judging by the strength of the sun through the curtains.

As I jump out of bed, I feel invigorated. This place has a habit of doing that to me and as I sweep aside the curtains, I see the twinkling bay set before me with the promise of a glorious day ahead.

I quickly dress in the clothes I was wearing the day before and head outside looking for the bathroom. There are no en-suite facilities in Perivale it would seem and I glance briefly at Jack's door as I pass, wondering if he's up yet.

Luckily, the bathroom's unoccupied, so I set about washing the sleep from my eyes and brushing my teeth with my finger and some toothpaste in the holder on the windowsill.

Groaning, I look at the person I became in the night. I may feel great inside but my face sorely disagrees. My eyes look bloodshot and pinched and there's a pallor to my cheeks that was created by the wine draining every ounce of colour from it. There are shadows under my eyes and my hair looks as if it needs a return visit to that hairdressers.

There's nothing for it but to swing it up into a ponytail and splash some water on my face to shock it back to life. Great, now I have to face everyone looking like the bride of Dracula.

Once I'm downstairs, I can see I'm alone. Bert and Sheila's car has gone which can only mean they are early risers and headed home to normality. The patio door is ajar, so I head outside blinking in the sunshine.

Once again, the view takes my breath away and not just because two extremely fit men are jogging up the sea path towards me. Jack and Max have obviously been swimming because the sea runs off their bodies like rivers of pure joy – for me, anyway. Either that or they sweat a lot.

They are wearing swimming trunks that draw my eye where I definitely shouldn't be tempted and the sight of their toned bodies make me weaker than I was just a few minutes ago.

Max spies me and calls out, "Hey, Rachel. Fancy a swim? I'll take you if you want."

Furiously pushing away the image of Max 'taking me', I smile with some relief. "Sorry, I didn't bring my cossie."

He grins wickedly. "Who needs one? I won't look, I promise."

Jack snorts. "Don't believe a word he says, Rachel, he can't be trusted."

Max grins and I shake my head. "I can think of another reason."

They look at me with puzzled expressions and I laugh. "Jellyfish."

Jack laughs. "Not on this side of the bay. Sorry to say, they prefer your side of it. If you need a swim, the only place in these waters is Max's private beach."

Max laughs. "Yes, strictly no Jellyfish allowed. I have a strict no Jellyfish policy here and have set border controls accordingly."

Jack rolls his eyes. "I think mother nature did that without your help."

They walk with me back inside and I say, "Where's Sally? Did she leave with Bert and Sheila?"

Max laughs. "She was sleeping like a baby when I got up. Knowing Sally, she'll surface at lunchtime and think it's still morning."

Jack nods and I feel a little surprised. As Max heads off to change Jack laughs at my expression. "You know, Rachel, you really should do something about the fact all your emotions show on your face. I can read you like a book."

"What do you mean?"

He grins. "You think Sally slept with Max last night, don't you?"

I feel a little silly and shake my head. "Well, maybe but it's just the way he said it."

Jack lowers his voice to a whisper. "Well, they did."

He laughs at my shocked expression.

"They always do, but not in the way you think. Max likes company, and he doesn't mind how he gets it. If it's not Sally, it's me. I think it goes back to his training. He's so used to sharing his room with a bunch of guys he feels strange sleeping alone. Like I said before, it's why we come up here. It's not just to see our friend but to make him feel at home. He likes sleeping with Sally because she lets him close. If he tried to pull me against him and sleep holding me, he'd get a black eye. Sally likes the comfort herself and they keep each other company. It's quite sweet, really."

We walk into the house and I try not to notice his toned, fit, body beside me. Since when did I turn into this wanton woman? I was never really that bothered before. Not that Spencer tended to walk around without his usual lounging pyjamas on in the flat. He even wore them in bed and I'm wondering what that says about our relationship? Not that I can talk, my fleecy PJs are the stuff of legends. No silky nightwear for me. Practical all the way and I am fast realising we had already turned into that old married couple before we even tied the knot.

As we head into the kitchen, I see Sally sitting at the table wearing one of Max's t-shirts. This one says 'Rocketman'.

She smiles and rubs her eyes sleepily. "Hey, guys. Why are you up so early?"

I laugh. "It's lunchtime Sally."

She shrugs. "Oh, is it? What are we having then?"

Jack laughs. "Who knows? Anyway, I'll go and shower and change and then maybe we can decide."

As he turns to leave, I say quickly, "I almost forgot, Jack, where's Millie?"

He smiles. "At my parents' house. They said they'd have her this weekend because when Max is home things get a little crazy."

Feeling slightly relieved that she's ok, I catch Sally looking at me strangely.

"What?"

She shakes her head and her lips twitch in a knowing smile. "You like him, don't you?"

"Who?"

She rolls her eyes. "Jack, of course. I mean, who wouldn't?"

I laugh a little hysterically. "Of course, I like him - as a friend. Honestly, Sally, you're mad. I'm here to forget about men not load my life up with another. Goodness me, whatever next? Ok, I'll give you that he's hot. I mean, in a boy next door, marriage material kind of way, and of course, he's handy with his hands and everything. Who wouldn't like a man as capable as he is alongside the good looks and hot body? Oh no, Sally, you've got it wrong if you think that sexy smile does things to me that it shouldn't. For goodness sake, how would I be interested in a man I've just met who I feel as if I've known all my life? Oh, what am I going to do with you, Sally? You are so wrong in every way possible and the thought of me and Jack, oh well… um… what can I say… is it hot in here?"

I grab a glass of water from the sink and down it in one as Sally smirks. "I thought so."

I can feel my cheeks growing increasingly warmer as I fail to hide my interest in her friend. What's happening to me? My life is spiralling out of control and I don't know where it will take me next. She says with interest.

"What happened with Logan Rivers?"

Spinning around, I almost choke on the water I suddenly want to douse myself in.

"What? Nothing as it happens. He needed a date for a boring dinner and I owed him for rescuing me from the Jellyfish. That's all, nothing to see there."

She says dreamily, "He's interesting, though, isn't he?"

Thinking of the surly, enigmatic, Mr Rivers, I roll my eyes. "If you like the brooding alpha male that completely rubs you up the wrong way and tramples on your principles, then yes, maybe he is interesting."

She looks a little lost and says sadly, "I like interesting people. They, well… interest me. I just wish I could meet one sometimes."

I look at her in surprise. "Well, I can think of a few around here you know very well. In fact, I'm pretty sure you just spent the night with one."

She laughs softly. "Max is the definition of interesting, I'll give you that. He's also more like my brother, so I think of him in a slightly different way."

Sitting down, I look at her keenly. "Would you ever consider a relationship with him? I mean, you are so well suited and obviously care for each other a great deal."

Sally laughs loudly. "Ugh. Never. It would be wrong on every level. Max and I are too similar. We understand each other and can finish each other's sentences. We know what the other one's thinking before they do and if he wasn't in my life, it wouldn't be complete. But, beyond that well…"

"Well, what?"

She sighs. "I want the fairy tale, Rachel. I want the Prince to rescue me from the tower and I want a man to bring out the woman in me. I don't want a man I can put on like a pair of well-worn favourite slippers. I want someone to see beyond the freakiness in me and understand there's a woman waiting to be discovered. I want that excitement you read about when the woman meets a man and she can't think of anything else. Is that possible for me? I doubt it because men don't see girls like me. They don't see us for all the pretty ones blinding them to the rest of us. When you don't conform to a stereotype, life can get a little less rosy. There is a lot of prejudice out there and I refuse to become something I'm not just to play the game. I want someone to see me for who I really am, not a manufactured version of what a woman thinks a man desires."

Reaching across, I grasp her hand and squeeze it tightly. "You'll find one, Sally. You just need to go out a little more and drop your guard. Maybe we should both head out one night and see where it takes us."

Before she can answer, Max charges into the room like one of the aircrafts he flies. "Ladies, ladies, you can relax because I'm back and ready to party again. How about I rustle you up the Max brunch special? Bacon, eggs, fries and all the trimmings."

My stomach growls hungrily which is all the answer he needs. Pulling Sally from her chair, he says lightly, "Come on, babe, you can be my sous chef. I need someone to order around and you'll do nicely"

I laugh as they start cooking and argue over everything. Shaking my head, I wish they could both see themselves how others see them. They are so right together and it's almost criminal they aren't a couple. I wonder how I can change their view of one another?

♥

Much later, Jack walks me home. Sally stays to keep Max company and after promising to meet them later for drinks in Pembury, I find myself heading down the little track to Bluebell cottage. Jack is good company and we find many things to chat about on the way.

As we reach the pretty cottage, I smile warmly and invite him in. He shakes his head ruefully. "Sorry, I would love to stay for a while but I have a job in Pembury I promised to complete. It will only take a couple of hours and then I need to check on Millie. I promised to have tea with my parents before we head out for drinks later. I'll come and pick you up if you like."

Fighting back the disappointment, I just smile. "That's fine. I said I'd drive, so Max and Sally can have a drink. It's silly dragging you all the way here when you live in Pembury. I'll see you later."

He smiles and yet somehow stays rooted to the spot. Both of us just looking at the other not quite sure what to say. Then he shakes his head awkwardly and grins. "Well, I guess I should be going?"

I smile. "Yes, I shouldn't keep you from your day."

He leans forward and my heart flutters as he lowers his face to mine and kisses me gently on the cheek. The feel of his breath on my face has me holding my breath and I involuntarily sway a little closer. He whispers, "I'll look forward to seeing you later, Rachel. Thanks, for a lovely evening."

Resisting the urge to pull him close and latch on to those sexy lips, I just say shyly, "Me too. Drive carefully."

As he walks down the path with a little wave, my heart runs rings around me as my head tells it to settle down already. My heart is telling me one thing and my head is telling me to sort my life out before complicating it any further. Sighing, I succumb to what my head tells me. I need to sort things out with Spencer before even thinking about starting anything with someone else.

♥16

As I open the door a white envelope sitting on the mat catches my attention. My heart jumps a little as the worry takes hold. They've found me!

It must be from home because who else would write to me here?

I pick the envelope up with shaking fingers and face the fear inside. As I draw out the note I see no name at the bottom. Wandering over to the settee, I perch on the edge and read with interest what's inside.

I am writing with information I think you should know. I don't want to get involved but can't remain silent.

It's common knowledge that Christopher Masters is intending to build a golf course near Perivale. He is looking for investors to fund his dream and nearly has the capital he requires.

What isn't common knowledge – yet, are his plans involving Perivale.

He is currently in talks to purchase the homes in the area. They sit on the edge of the proposed development and are the prime location for the new hotel he wants to build. He is also hopeful that when the plans become common knowledge, Bayside Manor will voluntarily sell to him rather than have the development on its doorstep.

He plans to gain the necessary planning permission by promising to re-build the village hall and provide the local area with a new shop and café on the beach.

I would hate to see this go ahead and wanted to warn you in advance. I'm not sure what you can do – if anything but hope you have a solution up your sleeve because I would hate to see the area spoiled in the name of profit and greed.

Please forgive my anonymity but I can't be seen to take sides.

Just for a moment time stands still. The words on this page are shocking on so many levels. The tears form as I think of the perfect little jewel that threatens to be tarnished by progress and greed. This is too much to take in and I sit back in shock. I'm not actually sure what to do and so decide on a walk to clear my head.

As if on autopilot, I find myself heading down to the beach. This time I don't register the serenity of the place. I feel angry on its behalf and wonder why business always has a hand in destroying things that were perfect before. Then I picture the people who I now call friends. Bert and Sheila, happy to retire here and Sally hiding from the world in a safe paradise. I wonder how easy it would be for Christopher Masters to buy their homes from under them. I know Sally rents hers but thought that Bert and Sheila owned theirs. I'm pretty sure they would refuse to sell, but knowing how these things work, I'm guessing if enough money is held out in temptation, they would be fools to resist.

As I reach the bay, I almost weep when I picture it filled with tourists and the hustle and bustle that comes with it. I suppose it's inevitable that things will change, after all, why not let more people enjoy this little piece of heaven? Maybe it's selfish of me but I don't care. If I can do anything to stop this, I will. Just how I can, is still a mystery.

It feels as if I walk for hours just thinking about the letter and when I look up, I don't recognise where I am. I appear to have rounded the bay to a very different type of beach. This one is more rugged and surrounded by rocks with none of the smooth sand of Perivale. The waves crash to the shore angrily and I see discarded debris washed up on the beach as if shipwrecked.

Then I see a house set back on a ridge. This house is impressive and it flashes angrily as its windows catch the sunlight. Made from steel and mirrors this house advertises everything about modern life. I'm guessing the house before it was old and worn. Probably bulldozed to make way for change and yet, despite this, the house that glares imperiously out to sea is magnificent.

I notice a little wooden walkway leading from the beach into landscaped gardens and wonder who lives here. Then I hear a terse, "Can I help you?"

As I look up, the penny drops as I see an angry Logan Rivers striding towards me, yelling, "Didn't you see the signs stating this is private property?"

Placing my hands on my hips, I say angrily, "I might have known you'd live here, and for your information, no, I didn't see a sign warning me to stay away. In fact, if I had, I would have gladly given you a wide berth because quite frankly I have a lot more on my mind than spending any time with you."

As I speak my harsh words, he draws near just as a seagull dive bombs me from a great height. Shrieking, I try to bat it away and he starts to laugh. "I should have known it was you, Rachel. Trouble seems to follow you when you venture outside that little cottage of yours. So, to what do I owe the honour of your visit?"

Still dodging the seagull who appears to have some sort of misguided premise that I'm food, I say angrily, "I'm not visiting, trespassing or anything else for that matter. I'm just taking a freaking walk, so call the cops and have me arrested."

He starts to laugh and before I know what's happening walks across and grabs my hand, spinning me into his chest and throwing his arms around me before starting up the beach to his house.

I squeal in a strangely muffled voice, "What are you doing, let me go?"

He says irritably, "Saving you again, of course. I've never known anyone so accident prone in my life. Don't you know anything about living with nature? You townies are all the same."

I beat my hands in fury on his hard chest which appears to do little to move the rock holding me so firmly.

Then I hear a door slam and I'm released into a large light-filled room that dazzles me completely.

All of my anger evaporates as I look at the amazing interior. It must be as big as Bluebell cottage in its entirety and is made up of cream settees and rugs, surrounded by chrome and glass. A wood burner sits in the corner and I can imagine how cosy this must be on a wild, wet, day, safely watching the storm outside in front of a raging fire.

Totally ignoring my captor, I wander around in awe. This is more like it. This is what I'm used to. High end gadgets, sumptuous furnishings, every luxury man can buy, framed by amazing artwork.

For once I'm speechless as Logan hands me a crystal glass filled with an amber liquid and says forcefully, "Drink this. It will settle those nerves of yours."

As if on autopilot, I do as he says and feel the liquid burn a trail to my bones.

As I catch his eye, his smirk knocks me back to my senses and I stare at him angrily. "I might have known you'd live here. Even the coastline changed into something harsh and unwelcoming."

He looks pleased. "Yes, I like that characteristic of it. It doesn't attract, it repels. Nobody wants to venture past the stones and inhospitable obstacles thrown in their path and just retreat to the pretty bay that lives next door."

He smirks as he raises his glass as if in a toast and I glare at him.

"So, you're back then."

He rolls his eyes. "Stating the obvious. Yes, as you can see, I'm back."

I feel the anger I've been holding building inside and snap, "Well, good. Maybe you should just turn around and head right back out of here again. I'm guessing you're celebrating tonight with your pal Christopher Masters on a job well done."

He looks surprised. "What are you talking about? He's no pal of mine, I thought I made that perfectly clear. Maybe you had better sit down and tell me what the problem is?"

Sighing, I sink down into – and I mean into – the squashy cream settee and wonder if I'll make it out alive. Sighing, I pull the letter from my pocket and hand it to him.

"Here you are, read this. It says it all."

I watch as he absorbs the words and frowns. "Who sent this?"

I roll my eyes. "There's no signature, Sherlock, so how am I frigging well supposed to know? Don't you know what anonymous means?"

He nods. "Of course, I do, but you must know who sent it, it's obvious."

I sigh loudly. "Then why ask me if it's obvious? Go on, tell me, so I can applaud your quick mind and keen detection skills."

He grins. "Why, it's Miriam, of course. I'm pretty certain of it. She's the only other person you spoke to that night, unless that man beside you took a shine to you without you knowing."

Shivering at the mere thought of that man, I have to agree he's probably right.

"But why would she go against her own family to tell me? It doesn't make sense."

He looks thoughtful. "I agree. So, what are you going to do about it?"

I stare at him gloomily. "I don't know. I suppose I should tell the other residents. I mean, it's more their fight than mine."

"Why?"

"Why, what?"

"Why is it more their fight than yours? After all, you live there too, so it will affect you."

I shake my head. "I'm staying there, Logan but I don't live there. I'm just trying to work out what I want and whether I should just head home and make the best of a bad situation."

He looks at me angrily. "I didn't have you down as a defeatist, Rachel."

I shrug. "I don't care what you had me down as. I'm in a strange situation of my own making. I turned my back on everything to come here and 'hashtag' discover what I want and I'm no further forward with that. How can I make a snap decision in just a few days, against a lifetime of memories in London? My entire future was planned there. Marriage, good job, a fabulous apartment and friends who were like-minded individuals who shared the same vision as I did. The trouble is, I'm not sure I share it anymore. I suppose I must have doubted it for some time which is why I took off so easily."

Logan hands me another drink and I grin. "What's this, getting me drunk so I'm at your mercy?"

He laughs softly. "I've never had to get a lady drunk to be at my mercy. She goes there willingly."

Suddenly, the heat in the room intensifies as I see the brooding individual looking at me from across the room. Suddenly, I notice the swell of his chest and the muscles flexing in his arms. I see the heat of his gaze and the intent in his eyes. Do I want, Logan? In this moment you can bet your whisky drinking, seagull dodging, woman in me, I do. What woman wouldn't be seduced by all this?

I sense a change in the atmosphere and suddenly it's serious as Logan stares at me as if working out his options. This man is an enigma and I can't read him. I shift awkwardly in my chair and my breathing intensifies as he moves across the room towards me. Reaching down, he plucks the glass from my hands and puts it on a nearby table. I almost can't breathe as he takes my hand and pulls me from the couch that lets me into his care willingly. He runs his hand around my waist and pulls me into his body. I can feel his hard-taut chest against mine as he lightly runs his finger down my face and says huskily, "Do you want me to kiss you, Rachel?"

I stare into those dark eyes that sparkle with lust. I feel my heart pushing me towards him and my head pulling it back. I lick my lips and imagine the taste of the man holding me so firmly in his arms and then I picture the man who is never far from my thoughts. Shakily, I whisper, "No."

He releases me immediately and smirks. "There's your answer."

I feel almost dizzy as I say, "What?"

He shrugs. "You're not ready to move on."

I stare at him incredulously. "What, you think that was the best test, are you mad? Just because I can resist your charm you think my heart's back in London. Well, newsflash, buddy, I don't need a man in my life to make it whole. Maybe I decided I didn't want one, full stop. Maybe I came here to escape from one and have decided I'd rather wait for the fairy tale like Sally."

He raises his eyes and I gaze at him furiously. "Yes, the fairy tale. What's wrong with that? Some women do actually want Prince Charming, you know. Someone to sweep them off their feet and make their life have meaning. Somebody who loves them above all else and makes it their mission in life to make their dreams come true."

I take a few deep, calming, breaths and say slowly, "Anyway, what has kissing you got to do with saving Perivale?"

He laughs. "Nothing. I just wondered that's all."

I stare at him incredulously. "You wondered? So, all that was a test to see if I could resist you. You're one sick individual if that's how you get your kicks."

He laughs and walks back to his seat across the room.

"Anyway, what are you going to do about it?"

My anger evaporates when faced with a bigger problem.

"I don't know. I'm meeting the others tonight for a drink in Pembury. Maybe we can come up with a plan together."

He nods and looks at me thoughtfully.

"Would you like some moral support? I can probably help if it's not too distracting for you."

He grins and I relax inside. This man confuses me in every way possible. I never know what he's thinking and yet strangely he puts me at ease and I feel I can trust him. So, I smile and grab the letter.

"Great, we're meeting at 7.30. I'm driving Max and Sally. You can hitch a ride with us if you like?"

He shakes his head. "You're joking, aren't you? I wouldn't trust you to drive a dodgem car. No, I'll drive you all, so at least we have one less problem to deal with."

As I prepare my retort, he winks and I breathe out instead. Then I toss my hair like a petulant child and head outside tentatively, looking for killer seagulls all the way home.

♥17

Logan is bang on time as usual and I hate the fact that my heart beats a little faster when I see him standing in the doorway of Bluebell cottage.

I invite him in while we wait for the others and he looks around with interest. "This place is probably worth a fortune. Not the building, quite honestly, I'd bulldoze it and build a brand new modern new build with every mod con going in its place. No, the real value in this property is that view. Its location's outstanding and I can see why Christopher Masters thinks a hotel would do well here."

I look at him angrily. "Well, for your information, I love this place. I adore every squeaky floorboard, every rusting pipe and every threadbare cushion. This place has character and history sewn together by many happy memories and I wouldn't change a thing."

I glare at him as he laughs softly. "What, not even fit a new kitchen with a dishwasher?"

I shake my head vigorously. "Nope."

"What, even a few new furnishings to make things more comfortable?"

"Not a chance."

He grins. "Not even a landscape garden to make the most of the outside space."

"Not in a million."

He raises his eyes. "You're delusional, Rachel. You're fooling yourself with an ideal. This place may call to the romantic in you but you try living here 24/7, 365 days a year. You would soon crave the modern conveniences that were designed to make life easier. I'm guessing it would all change then."

I hate to admit that he's probably right and just say gloomily. "That's the trouble, isn't it, Logan? We all want the perfect life. We want the past to sit alongside the present giving us the best of what's been with the best available now. You're right, Bluebell cottage does need a radical overhaul. The trouble is, in doing so it will tear a little piece of its charm away. I wonder what the solution is?"

He doesn't have time for another snarky comment before there's a loud knock on the door.

I run to answer it with relief and see Sally and Max standing there looking a little worried.

I usher them in and watch Sally almost have a panic attack as she sees Logan watching them.

Max looks surprised as I say, "Sally, Max I'm not sure if you've met Logan before."

Sally shakes her head, almost hyperventilating, as Max shakes his hand vigorously. "Good to meet you, though a little surprised."

Sally smiles shyly and I watch Logan look at her incredulously. I smile to myself as she is very pretty in pink tonight. Her hair is now pale pink and compliments her baby pink dress. She is wearing jewelled sandals and holding a sparkling clutch. Dare I say it, she seems almost normal tonight, and I'd like to think Max was responsible for the sparkle in her eye.

She almost hides behind him as Logan continues to stare at her broodingly. Then Max holds out a similar letter to mine and says harshly, "Read this, Rachel. Sally got one and so did Bert & Sheila."

I produce mine with a flourish and look at them despondently.

"What do you think?"

Max sighs. "I think we've got a problem. The most pressing one is the fate of Bluebell and Honeysuckle cottages. They are owned by third parties who may be susceptible to a deal."

He turns to Sally. "Who did you say you rent from, babe?"

She says in a small voice. "Princeton holdings. They're a property investment company."

I sigh heavily. "Great. Money talks in those cases so they'll probably sell out first."

Max looks annoyed. "I'm guessing they're in touch with the Steepleheads as well. No doubt offering to pay Molly's care bills and promising an inflation grabbing sum for the deeds on this place."

Logan says harshly, "So, what do you propose we do about it?"

Max looks surprised. "We?"

Logan nods. "Listen, I own the beach house in the next bay and the last thing I want is a horde of interfering tourists tearing up my coastline and I'm pretty sure you share that view. So, we need to act and stop this before it gets out of hand."

I say with exasperation. "What can we do? We're small fry compared to big business."

Logan's eyes flash. "Think about it. The letter said it was buying up these properties. We make that difficult. Secondly, they haven't got planning permission yet for the hotel, which hinges on providing a better village hall and shop and café. Why don't we organise events to raise money to remodel the village hall ourselves and install a café in there? That way the reason for granting the permission will be obsolete."

Sally's eyes widen and she says in a whisper, "But that will take hundreds and thousands of pounds. No amount of jumble and cake sales will generate that sort of money."

Logan shrugs. "Then use what you all have between you and use your talents to save Perivale.

I'm guessing you could all contribute something worthwhile to the cause. Maybe I can get the ball rolling."

We look at him expectantly. "I've just been to London to attend talks about my new computer game. I have three interested parties who would agree to any condition I make in order to secure the rights. I'm willing to make it a condition they donate £50,000 to my chosen worthy cause. That will be small fry to them and will go a long way to starting the renovation project."

I think at this moment I love Logan Rivers. Max looks suitably impressed and Sally looks as if he just delivered the moon.

She says shakily, "I could auction off a painting. I have a couple I painted of the bay from Bayside manor last year. They're quite special to me but I'm willing to donate them to the cause."

Logan looks suitably impressed and I say with excitement. "That's fantastic, Sally. Are you sure though? I mean, if they're special, you should hold on to them."

She shakes her head. "It's fine, I can always paint another."

Max looks thoughtful. "I could get the guys to sign a few items and do a meet and greet at the village hall. We could sign autographs and let the kids take selfies with us."

Logan smiles and looks to me. "What about you, Rachel?"

I shake my head slowly. "Let's just say I've had a very interesting idea on how to help but it involves quite a few other factors if it's going to work."

They look at me with interest and I smile. "I'll tell you if it all works out. In the meantime, we have an evening out to enjoy. Shall we head off?"

As I turn the key to lock Bluebell cottage, I feel the weight of its future on my hands and vow not to let it down whatever happens.

♥18

Logan drives us to Pembury in a large black Range Rover. I can tell the others are slightly intimidated by him and I don't blame them. He's certainly a force unto himself and as I sit beside him, I don't even try to make polite conversation. The others sit in the back and occasionally I catch Sally smiling at Max as he gives her hand a squeeze.

We park up fairly easily and make our way to the local pub, The Bayside Inn. The place is heaving and yet it appears that all conversation stops as we make our way inside. To be honest, I'm not surprised. Logan Rivers is something of a celebrity around here and rarely ventures into town. Then there's their very own celebrity, Max. The Red Arrows daredevil that has the women standing a little taller and throwing him suggestive looks.

Then we see Jack and my heart skips a beat. He's leaning on the bar chatting to a couple of girls who lean into him as if to hear his words better. I feel a flash of irritation as they laugh at something he says and watch as he grins that sexy grin and appears to be enjoying himself. Then he looks up and our eyes meet and everything else fades away. He holds my gaze and then whispers something to the girls hanging onto his every word before moving towards us. To my surprise, he nods at Logan and smiles. "Good to see you, Logan. Surprised though."

Logan smiles. "Me too, Jack. You have our newest villager to thank for the invitation."

Jack looks between us and I notice a little of the sparkle leave his eyes. He turns his attention to Max who whispers, "We've got terrible news. Let's find a corner to sit and we'll fill you in."

As we head to the far reaches of the pub, I'm wondering if this is really the best place to discuss this? It may be best to park the problem and just concentrate on having a good night.

I watch as Jack reads the note and frowns. His gaze darts between us and he says in a low voice. "Do you know who sent this?"

Logan leans in. "We think it may be Miriam Masters."

Sally gasps. "Surely not. Why would she do that?"

I whisper, "I saw her in the store the other day and she asked me if you were going to invest, Logan. I said I didn't know, and she told me she hoped you weren't. Then she ran off back to the office without explaining why."

Max says softly, "I say we find Miriam and find out everything she knows."

Jack whispers, "How are we going to do that? Her father watches her every move, she's never allowed out."

Sally says quietly, "I know she goes to help out at the village hall when its bridge club. Her mother runs it and Sally's made to run around making tea and serving biscuits. Maybe Sheila can help?"

Max looks thoughtful. "You know, it doesn't change the facts. We need to work out how we can re-model the village hall, somehow stop people from selling the cottages and raise public awareness without dropping Miriam in it."

We all sit back gloomily. I look across at Sally and say, "When did you say you were visiting Molly?"

She smiles. "Tuesday."

Jack looks at me and smiles. "Do you fancy some company, Sally? Do you think Molly would mind two more?"

I stare at him gratefully as Sally looks surprised. "I'm sure she would love to see you, why, what's your plan?"

I sit back and say sadly, "I'm not sure but we need to get our point across. If Molly loves that place as much as I think she does, I'm pretty sure she will be devastated to learn of its possible fate. Who knows, maybe she can help us?"

We are interrupted by a group of young girls who crowd around Max asking for selfies with him. Of course, he obliges and as I watch him in action, I take a look across to see Sally's reaction. However, Sally isn't even looking as her attention is firmly fixed on one very domineering, insufferable, enigmatic sex god, Logan. They are chatting away as if they've known each other for years and I stare in amazement as she giggles at something he says and watch a soft expression cross his face. I look over at Jack who grins and then winks before shifting seats to the one vacated by Max. Leaning down, he whispers, "Well, that's a surprise."

I look at him in shock. "I can't believe Sally's so animated. I thought she'd be scared stiff of Logan but look at her, she's really enjoying herself, and so is he."

Jack looks concerned, "Do you mind?"

I laugh. "Mind what? If they get on, good for them. I'm not interested in Logan Rivers, Jack. I can't believe you thought I was."

He sits back and watches Max field off the advances of the groupies and I think about what he's said. Am I bothered? I'm annoyed to realise that I am; although why, is a mystery.

As evenings go this one is up there with the best. The company is excellent and the venue cosy and welcoming. I enjoy sitting beside Jack and watching the struggle between Max and his feelings.

Once the groupies drifted away, I watched him fixate on Sally and Logan. He tried to hide it but every time Sally laughed, I saw his eyes dart across sharply. He tried to cover it up by telling loud jokes and stories that included Sally, hoping to divert her attention back to him. Jack caught my eye several times and smiled with amusement. When Jack headed to the bar for more drinks, Max took his seat and whispered, "Do you think Logan likes Sally?"

I look across and see him laugh at something she says and say slowly, "They seem to be getting on. Why do you ask?"

He stares at his drink moodily. "I just don't want her hurt."

I say gently, "Are you sure that's all that's bothering you?"

He looks up and shakes his head. "Of course. Sally's family to me and I look out for her. If I think she's going to be made a fool of or hurt in any way, of course, I'll try my best to stop it."

I shrug and hide a smile. Then he says in a strangely lost voice, "Do you think she'll still come home with me tonight?"

I look at him in surprise. "Why wouldn't she if you arranged it?"

He appears to perk up a little. "Of course, she wouldn't let me down."

Leaning closer, I whisper, "Why can't you stay there by yourself?"

He looks a little sad. "I hate it, Rachel. I'm used to lots of noise and conversation. I love coming home but it's not the same when you're alone. I've always been the same. I need company, always have and usually the female kind. What can I say, I attract them like bees to pollen? Then there are my mates. We're together 24/7 in the Air force and the Red Arrows is the same tight unit. When I come home, I leave all that behind me. I can't start anything with anybody because I'm here so infrequently. That's why I need Sally and Jack. They provide life in my house so I don't stay away."

Once again, Sally laughs and I see a little piece of the sparkle in Max's eyes die. His shoulders slump and I reach out and grasp his hand. "Loneliness is a terrible thing, Max. We are very alike you and me. We both want something we don't believe we can have. There is too much responsibility on our shoulders and too many people to take into consideration. I'm guessing that if you found one person to make a life with, you would be happier for it. A family of your own that moves where you go. The trouble is, you are resisting what's right in front of your face because you don't think it's the right thing for the person you love. That's a noble sacrifice, Max but a foolish one. If it's meant to be then it will happen. Don't sacrifice your happiness out of fear of the unknown."

He leans across and says softly, "Ditto, Rachel."

We share a smile as Jack heads back with the drinks. I watch as Logan excuses himself and Max jumps into his seat quicker than he can fly. Jack hands me my drink and grins. "Jealousy is a powerful weapon."

I nod. "So, it would seem. Do you think she knows?"

Jack smiles at them fondly. "Not a clue. That's Sally for you; so wrapped up in her own little world she only sees the magic. She doesn't see the obvious and wouldn't believe you if you told her."

Logan returns and sits next to me and smiles. "So, you have a plan at least. I'll honour my end of the bargain and now it's up to you to face your fears."

Jack looks confused as I share a smile with Logan. Yes, this is one fear that will affect many more people than me. To be honest, I'm not sure I'm ready for it.

♥19

The next morning, I head to Bert and Sheila's to see if they've had a letter. Sheila is baking some sweet-smelling scones and my mouth waters as she places one before me.

Bert materialises out of thin air just as the scones are ready and we sit around their kitchen table to discuss a plan of action.

Sheila looks at me with a frown. "You know, when I saw that letter, I told Bert if they so much as set a foot in Perivale I'll let them feel the sharp edge of my tongue. I mean, how dare they play with people's lives like this as if we don't matter."

I stare out of the window gloomily. "We don't matter, Sheila. In the grand scheme of things, we are like a tiny grain of sand on that fabulous beach outside. I'm not sure if we can stop the inevitable but we should at least try."

Bert nods. "That's right, Rachel. Don't let the buggers win. It's the British way you know. We stand tall and proud in the face of adversity."

Sheila rolls her eyes. "Since when have you stood tall and proud, Bert?"

He smiles with smug satisfaction. "I was in the army cadets for two weeks once. I only left because it interfered with my social life."

Sheila shakes her head. "I'm in awe of your commitment, Bert. I'm not sure they ever recovered from the loss."

Laughing, I take another bite of the scone as Sheila says firmly. "Well, they won't get our cottage, not for all the teas in China. They could offer us millions of pounds and I wouldn't budge. They would have to build the hotel around us because I'm staying put."

Bert nods and I shake my head. "I'm not sure if they can affect a compulsory purchase. If they do, you are likely to get less than what they offer you in the first place."

Sheila looks shocked. "What, they could take our home, anyway?"

I feel bad as I see the worry in her eyes and smile reassuringly. "I doubt that would happen. No, there must be something we can do."

As Bert and Sheila sit there despondently, I say casually, "Does that offer still stand of showing me how a bridge club works?"

Sheila looks surprised. "Of course, in fact, we are meeting this afternoon. Would you like to come?"

I smile gratefully. "Yes please, Sheila. In fact, I can't think of anywhere I would rather be today."

Later that afternoon, I find myself walking down the hill with Sheila towards the village hall. As we approach, I take in the dilapidated edges and crumbling wood. The inside isn't much better and years of use have culminated in a mismatched jumble of tables, chairs and an odd smell that has built up over the years. I dread to think of the state of the kitchen as I see the serving hatch open and Miriam gaily serving the players with tea and biscuits.

I shiver as I see Sophia Masters gazing around her imperiously, ticking names off a register. As she sees me accompanying Sheila her eyes narrow, and she sets her lips into a hard line.

Sheila pulls me over and says happily, "Room for one more, Sophia. This is Rachel my new neighbour who is keen to see how this all works."

Mrs Masters nods her head slightly and says in her clipped voice, "Welcome, dear. Maybe it would be best if you observed this afternoon. We are a serious club who have no time to teach. Maybe Sheila should teach you privately until you are of a standard."

Sheila rolls her eyes behind Sophia's back and I stifle a grin, nodding in agreement. "Of course, I fully understand."

She glides off to talk to another unfortunate soul and I edge my way to the serving hatch. Miriam looks up and smiles warmly. "Hi, Rachel. I never expected to see you here."

I laugh softly. "Me neither. Sheila offered so here I am."

She pushes a cup of tea towards me and offers me the plate of biscuits. "Here, help yourself. Have you ever played bridge before?"

I shake my head. "No, to be honest, I'm not really sure I want to learn."

Miriam nods. "Yes, it's never held much appeal for me. The trouble is, when your mother runs the local club you do sort of have to get involved."

I smile sympathetically as Sophia claps her hand and calls the room to attention.

"Ladies, ladies settle down. We need to begin if we are to make any headway. Observers may watch but no talking."

She stares pointedly at me and I just smile sweetly as I grab a little plastic seat and sit behind Sheila.

As I pretend to watch, I rack my brains how I can broach the subject with Miriam. I can't just blurt it out because what if she didn't send the note? I notice that she doesn't join in and just tidies the kitchen, so after a while, I slip away and join her behind that archaic serving hatch.

She looks up as I enter the room and smiles. Grabbing a filthy tea towel that shouts in alarm for a public health enquiry, I start to dry the freshly washed cups and saucers. Miriam says in a whisper,

"How have you been settling in, Rachel? Have you met any of the locals yet?"

I nod. "Well, obviously I met Logan, then, of course, Sheila and Bert. I love my new neighbour Sally, she's a real character and I've just met Max. Oh, and of course, Jack, who was my knight in shining bath enamel when he installed a new one in Bluebell cottage."

She laughs softly. "That's Jack. He's most girls knight in shining armour around these parts."

Images of him chatting to the two girls last night come to mind and the alarm bells start ringing. "What is Jack a bit of a player around here?"

Miriam giggles. "Not by choice but in case you hadn't noticed, this place is quite small and any passable guy is usually in demand. Mind you, Jack was off the market when Fiona was around and the word is, she's heading home. Apparently, the bright lights weren't so bright after all and she misses this place – oh and Jack of course."

I actually feel sick as she continues. "I heard he never got over her and they'll probably pick up where they left off."

I smile shakily. "That's nice."

She throws me a cheeky smile and sighs. "Mind you, Jack is just a boy compared to Logan Rivers. That guy is all man and then some. You were lucky to get asked out by him on your first day."

I roll my eyes. "You call it lucky, I call it unlucky."

She looks at me with a shocked expression. "Why?"

I shake my head and laugh. "Well, he is rather opinionated and his manner could use a little work. I don't know why but I'm just not myself around him."

Miriam nods in agreement. "I understand how you feel because I'm the same. The man makes me forget how to form words. My words trip over themselves around him and so I keep them contained. Just one look is enough to make me forget my own name."

We grin and I say carefully, "So, how are things progressing with the golf course. Did your father get his investment?"

I watch as Miriam's hands shake slightly as she washes the next cup. She stares at the bowl and says in a small voice, "Almost."

I carry on testing. "So, when do you think the work will start?"

She shrugs. "I'm not sure. There's still a couple of items outstanding before they can go ahead."

"Oh, what are they?"

She almost freezes and then looks over her shoulder and whispers, "They need to secure some more land and then can make a start on the golf course."

I say in a low voice, "Do you think they'll get the land?"

She sighs, "I hope not."

I'm aware I don't have long before the players descend on us again, so say urgently, "Why not, Miriam?"

She smiles sadly. "Because if they do, a little piece of Perivale will be gone forever. Maybe it's disloyal of me but I would rather work with what we've got rather than change it. I'm of the opinion that progress doesn't always have to mean change. What my father wants is money, Rachel. He doesn't see the consequences of his actions and thinks he's doing this to secure the future of Perivale. The trouble is, I think it's his future he is considering above everything else, so, no, I don't want his plan to succeed."

The voices in the room outside get louder, signalling the end of the game and I say urgently, "Was it you who sent the letters, Miriam?"

I can tell she's surprised and looks around her fearfully. She whispers urgently, "If they knew I warned you my life would be hell. I did so because I couldn't sit back and watch them destroy such a magical place. Do what you can, Rachel because I would hate to see their plans fulfilled. Don't get me wrong, I think a golf course is a fabulous idea and would bring people and money into the area. However, what my father wants is more than that. He wants to turn Perivale into some kind of holiday destination that would just increase in size over the years. The coastline will be spoiled, and the beaches destroyed. The roads around here would choke with cars and our quiet idyllic life will be a thing of the past. You can call me selfish if you want and a dinosaur who is behind the times but we should preserve a little of the beauty of the past to appreciate the life before us. There are plenty of places crying out for investment but Perivale isn't one of them."

Quickly, Miriam sets about getting the cups ready and placing out another plate of biscuits. As I help, I think about what she said. All my life I've been surrounded by big business. The bottom line is the only line and what it takes to get us there has always been meticulously planned. It's ironic I now find myself on the other side of the fence and wonder what my father would say if he saw who I had become. Miriam and I are not so different, really. However, I am luckier in one sense. My father always wants what's best for me above everything else. If I had wanted to go abroad and work, he would have encouraged me. I didn't intend on working in the family business, it just happened by chance. Maybe it's time to stretch my own wings and try something new. Maybe this is my calling and I owe it to everyone to do what I do best, to preserve the past.

♥20

As I wait in Sally's crowded kitchen for Jack, I feel a little nervous. Today we are visiting Molly Steeplehead at the care home and I'm not sure what to expect. I'm a stranger to her who by rights shouldn't dare to visit. Luckily, Sally and Jack are not, so I've told Sally to go in first and ask if I can.

I mull over my conversation with Miriam but only one part of it's on repeat in my mind. Jack's girlfriend's coming home. I'm not sure why I feel so let down. It's not as if he's shown any interest in me, or me him for that matter. We've just become friends like he is with Max and Sally.

However, I can't ignore the looks we share and the feeling that something good is about to happen. Jack makes me feel settled and part of something but I don't know what? When he's with me I feel complete. It's as if he was always meant to be by my side, yet now that will never happen.

Mind you, who am I kidding? I'm an engaged woman with more emotional baggage than she can carry. I'm not a free woman to indulge in such fantasies and there's the little fact of life back in London to consider. Jack would be wise to keep his distance and I should do the same.

Maybe I should just use Logan for sex instead. I'm not lying the thought has crossed my mind on a few occasions. It would certainly be an experience. Maybe he's the man I should be with. I quite like his company and there's no denying the attraction we share. He also seems to understand me and knows just what I'm thinking. Despite his gruff exterior, I think he's hiding a softer side, evident by his generous offer to the village hall. Maybe I'm missing a trick with him.

Sally interrupts my rambling thoughts by floating into her kitchen in a lavender sundress with violet hair. "I think I'm ready, Rachel. I thought I'd pay homage to Bluebell cottage and make Molly feel at home."

"You look amazing, Sally. Molly will be pleased to see you."

She nods. "I'll be happier. It's great having you here, Rachel but I do miss her. She was full of stories that made me laugh and think in equal measure."

I watch as she carefully places the painting of Bluebell cottage in a paper bag and grabs a cake tin off the side. She sees me looking and smiles, "Lemon drizzle. Its Molly's favourite."

We hear a car pull up outside and Sally smiles. "It's Jack. Shall we head off?"

I see Jack exiting the car and my heart races a little faster. Just seeing the man does that to me and yet I can't allow it. I see Sally smirking and raise my eyes, "What?"

She lowers her voice. "You like him, don't you?"

I nod, "Of course, I do. What's not to like? In fact, I like you all."

She laughs. "You don't fool me, I know more when I see it and if it's any help, I would say he likes you too."

Jack calls out, "Your taxis here," and Sally grins.

"I'll sit in the back, I can hold on to the painting that way."

She laughs as I roll my eyes and follow her out.

My nerves settle as Jack smiles in that way he has of making the world right itself. He looks smart today in smart cargo shorts and a white linen shirt. He's the sort of guy who could wear anything and pull off the casual, chic, look of a man who doesn't have to try too hard. As we approach, I allow myself to wallow in that sexy look, pretending we are together in a much more satisfying way than friends. His eyes light up as he sees the cake tin and Sally laughs.

"Keep your hands off my buns, Jack, they're out of bounds."

We giggle as he rolls his eyes and grins. "Sally, there are not many people in this world who could keep their hands off your buns."

He adds slyly, "Including our supersonic friend who can't seem to stay away from you since he arrived."

Sally looks confused. "What, Max? I'm not sure what you mean."

Jack grins wickedly. "Maybe you should open your eyes a little, I think our friend has developed feelings for you."

Sally looks shocked. "You're wrong, Jack. Max is like a brother to me, nothing else."

Shrugging, he starts the engine. "What about a certain brooding neighbour of ours then, Logan Rivers? Maybe he's more your type."

Sally laughs nervously. "Oh, he's just being kind, I think he likes Rachel if I'm honest."

Jack turns to look at me sharply and I squirm with embarrassment. "Are you kidding, Sally? That man only loves himself. He's insufferable, rude and the angriest person I know. I obviously annoy him and he certainly does me. In fact, I'm sure the only person Logan Rivers has any time for is himself. Shutting himself away in his beach house, only venturing out to pick on innocent people who are just going about their day. Goodness, what an imagination you have, Sally. Logan Rivers, don't make me laugh."

Just for a moment, there's an awkward silence in the car. My heart is pounding with what I can only describe as irritation at the thought that Logan likes me. What on earth must Jack think? I'm acutely aware that what Jack thinks is more important to me than it should be. The lovely man driving us is everything I ever wanted when I thought of my future. Kind, funny with an easy personality that makes you feel happy inside. He's also jaw-droppingly handsome and the sort of man your mother would most certainly approve of. Someone who would fit in well with the family and would never let you down. Jack is the man I always thought I'd marry, not someone like Spencer who charms his way through life always looking for something better.

Thinking about Spencer, I remember how happy I was when he started paying me attention. He was charming, witty and attentive. He made me feel like a princess and I counted my lucky stars that he liked me too. He proposed over a candlelit dinner at the Savoy one night. It was so romantic and everything I had ever wished my proposal to be. Of course, I said yes and when he produced the Tiffany ring my world was complete.

I'm not sure when the doubts started. It was so gradual they sort of crept up on me. A whispered word in the ladies when nobody thought I was there, or a furtive phone call in the middle of the night. An irritated glance in my direction as I stole a kiss and the little digs here and there.

Gradually, our little bubble began to deflate, and the magic appeared to be the first thing to evaporate. All that was left was the day to day mundane living. The only words spoken were to decide what to eat that night and then what to watch on the television.

Sighing, I picture my life back in London. A regimented day where we would both head off to the same office, grabbing our usual coffees 'to go' on the way. There was little conversation on the train as we checked our phones and prepared ourselves for the day ahead. No words were spoken as we headed for our respective offices and our paths only crossed in the day if there was business to attend to. There were no little love messages designed to recharge the romance. No whispered phone calls that kept the flame burning. No secret rendezvous to keep the magic alive and no promises of a future where things would be different.

Sighing, I look out of the window as Sally says gently, "Is everything ok, Rachel, you've gone quiet on us? We were only teasing about Logan."

Shaking myself back to the present, I realise in horror they thought I was thinking about *him*. Feeling cross, I say shortly, "I wasn't thinking of Logan. I try not to if I'm honest, that man completely rubs me up the wrong way. No, I was thinking about life in London and the fool I left behind."

Jack says gently, "Do you miss London and … um… him?"

"Good God, no! I can't believe you'd think that. I was just remembering where it all went wrong. Distance makes things seem clearer somehow. When I look at my life there, it's not a patch on the one I wanted. I thought I had everything but coming here has shown me how poor I was where it counts. I suppose it's never far away from my thoughts though. I know I'll have to head back at some point and I'm dreading it."

Sally says loudly, "Then don't go back. You can make your life in Perivale. Get a job locally and set up home here. We'll help you, won't we, Jack?"

Jack nods and says with determination. "Of course, we will. Sally's right, Rachel. Stay here and let us look after you."

The little voice in my head shouts loudly. 'Not *we*, Jack, *you*. I want to hear, 'let *me* look after you,' and I want *you* to be the one to chase the shadows away.

I look at him in surprise as I realise what my heart has known for some time. Jack is the man of my dreams, the man who sets my soul on fire and the man worth fighting for and I would leave everything behind if I thought he felt the same.

The car stops at the traffic lights and he turns to smile at me. The look he sends me is a shared one. In his eyes, I see the same hope reflected back at me. I smile shyly and his eyes sparkle with an understanding. The look we share is a common one when two people want the same thing. Jack and Rachel, Rachel and Jack, yes, it sounds perfect. Jack is the man for me, I know it in my heart. Now I just need him to realise that and we can begin.

♥21

Applegarth House is an impressive building not far outside Pembury. It's a huge mansion house that dominates the skyline, sitting serenely on top of a hill with a spectacular view of the sea. Manicured lawns and beautiful gardens wrap around it and despite its age, it looks grand and well cared for.

As we drive to the car park, I see many workers pushing blanket-covered residents in their wheelchairs, out for some healing sunshine as Verity called it. As places go this one's not a bad one and my heart settles a little. At least Molly isn't in some dingy place where they just prop up the residents in front of a blaring television. I hope not anyway.

We walk towards the impressive doors and into a large hallway. I feel slightly nervous and whisper to Sally, "Maybe I should wait here until you say it's ok. I would hate to make Molly feel awkward."

Sally nods and Jack says sweetly, "I'll wait with Rachel. You go in first and come and get us when Molly's ready."

Sally smiles as a beaming woman approaches us. "Welcome, it's good of you to come. Which one of our lovely residents have you come to brighten their day?"

We smile at the friendly woman as Sally says, "Molly Steeplehead. She's expecting me but I brought two more visitors with me. They'll just wait here until I check it's ok with her first."

The lady smiles happily. "Oh, I'm sure she'll be only too happy to see you. I must say, we all love Molly. She's such a ray of sunshine and her stories are amazing. I don't get any work done when she's around. I could listen to her all day."

Sally nods. "That's Molly."

The woman smiles. "I'll take you to see her. She's in the conservatory, she likes it in there. The view of the sea is breath-taking, and she says she enjoys feeling the sun on her."

Jack grins. "Typical Molly."

We watch them leave and Jack says, "You know, when you spoke of your life in London it made me think."

I hold my breath as he says softly, "When you spoke of returning there it didn't seem right and I don't want you to go. I like having you around and I apologise if this sounds a little forward but it occurred to me that I may not have long, so here goes."

He looks into my eyes and says sweetly, "I like you, Rachel. I enjoy your company and look forward to seeing you. It's funny but for some reason, I can't stop thinking about you and I was wondering if you'd like to maybe... um... come on a date with me tonight? Not as friends, um... but maybe as something a little more?"

He looks so awkward standing there, I want to reassure him and smile happily, "I'd like that. It's funny, but I didn't come here looking for a man but I think about you a lot. I feel comfortable with you and as if I've always known you. Does that sound silly?"

He reaches out and takes my hand and I shiver inside. I can't stop smiling as he looks into my eyes with his extremely sexy ones and says softly, "No it doesn't. It sounds perfect. Like you, I wasn't looking for anything and swore off women for a while after Fiona left. I was hurt and thought I'd take some time out for a while. The trouble is, I can't stay away and may lose you if you are forced to return to London. I want to see where this feeling takes me because if I ignore it, I would be the fool, not the guy you spoke of."

I almost think he's going to kiss me right here in this geriatric paradise. Goodness, that would be a story for the grandchildren, but we are interrupted as Sally heads back quicker than we thought.

"Guys, Molly said come in and stop making the place untidy."

She grins as she sees Jack's hand in mine and her eyes flash with 'I told you so.' Grinning madly, we follow her and I'm happy that Jack's hand stays firmly clasped to mine.

Molly is sitting in a light-filled conservatory facing a view that takes my breath away. The lady we have come to see looks up and I watch her eyes sparkle with kindness and youth that her body betrays. Sally takes a seat beside her and she beckons Jack forward. "Jack, my darling. Come and give an old woman a hug and make her day."

I watch as he pulls her close and hugs her gently. She whispers something to him and as she pulls back, takes a long look at him and smiles. "Still the same gorgeous boy I've always loved."

She laughs softly and then looks at me with a curious smile. "You must be Rachel, the new guardian of Bluebell cottage. Come and sit by me and tell me tales of my home."

I do as she says, and she fixes me with a kind look. "I'm happy to meet you, dear. When my son told me he was renting the old place out I was a little worried. Firstly, because quite frankly the house is a mess and I couldn't imagine anyone actually wanting to live there. Secondly, because I wanted to think of someone who would love the place as much as I did, sorry, do."

I smile softly. "Your home is magical, Molly and I've never lived in such a fabulous place in my life. I love everything about it."

She rolls her eyes. "It's ok, dear. You don't have to love all my old tat. I mean, have you seen that bathroom? I must say, I was quite relieved to get here and have a nice bath for once."

Jack laughs. "Well, you'll be pleased to know that a new bath is currently taking pride of place in Bluebell cottage, courtesy of your son."

Molly's eyes soften. "I'm glad of that. It's actually a load off my mind because nobody should be forced to endure that nightmare every day."

She turns to Sally. "How about you dear girl? Have you been keeping busy?"

She whispers to me, "That's politely asking if she's brought me a cake."

I stifle a grin as Sally removes the tin with a flourish. "Here you are, Molly, your favourite just the way you like it."

I wonder if it's against the law to rugby tackle an old chair-ridden pensioner for a cake tin? Thinking better of it, I just stare at the cake jealously. Molly looks so happy it's as if Sally brought her the gift of eternal life. Her eyes soften and she says fondly. "You know, Sally, you have quite a gift for baking. You really should pursue it, it's a criminal act keeping it hidden."

Sally shrugs. "I prefer to paint. Speaking of which, I painted you this."

She removes the brown paper-wrapped package from the bag and holds it out to Molly. I say quickly, "Shall I hold the cake for you?"

Molly laughs. "Good try, Rachel. I may be old but I've still got all my marbles."

We all laugh as she places the tin on the table in front of her and takes the parcel from Sally. I watch her closely as she unwraps the picture and see the emotion in her eyes as she beholds her beloved home. I watch as she's transported back to a place with happy memories and where her dreams were made. She almost can't speak as she says in a whisper, "Thank you. This means the absolute world to me. I never thought I'd see it again and yet you have made sure I'll see it every day. Thank you, my dear."

Sally's tears mirror my own as she gently hugs the frail woman.

Molly stares at it long and hard and says softly, "Bluebell cottage was my home for most of my life. I was a married woman there, a mother and widower and a grandmother. I am also soon to be a great grandmother so the circle is complete."

She says almost breathlessly, "I may have come to the end of my time there but life goes on. I hope the next owner will cherish it as much as I did, sorry do, and give it some love to restore it to its former glory. I would hate to see it fall into ruin and nothing would give me greater pleasure than seeing it filled with a family once again. It's a place where children should grow and have a magical childhood. It's a family house that should have noise and chatter filling the rooms. The garden should be encouraged to bloom and grow and the windows sparkle with sunshine and happiness. That's what I want for Bluebell cottage."

I feel a huge lump in my throat as I picture its possible fate. Jack says gently, "I'm sorry, Molly but we have some alarming news concerning not just Bluebell cottage but your neighbours too."

Molly looks at him sharply, "Go on."

Jack sighs and produces the letter from his pocket. "Read this, it tells you everything you need to know."

I think I hold my breath as Molly places her glasses on the end of her nose and reads the letter carefully. I watch her hand shake and feel tormented by how she must be feeling. I know how I felt and I've just arrived. What must it feel like for the woman who loves it more than any of us?

When she reaches the end, she sighs sadly and removes her glasses. Shaking her head, she says bitterly, "I always knew this day would come. We live in a changing world and business dictates it. I'm just surprised it's taken this long."

Sally says gloomily, "What can we do, Molly? We have tried to think of ways to stop this and all we can think of is to restore the village hall by holding fundraisers and auctioning items. This is almost a losing battle from the start."

Molly smiles ruefully. "I once heard a saying that's always resonated with me. *When something is important enough, you do it even if the odds are not in your favour.* You owe it yourselves and the place you call home to at least try."

Jack says with desperation, "But how can we compete against this? The only thing we can do is to resist them every step of the way."

Molly looks at me and says softly, "What about you, Rachel? This isn't really your fight, yet here you are. Why is that?"

I share a look with Jack who smiles reassuringly. Sally nods and I say softly, "It's not my fight but it's one I very much want to win. When I came here, I was escaping a world I no longer wished to live in. Business has been a large part of my life and has been good to me. The trouble is, I've discovered it doesn't fulfil me. I am disillusioned with the choices I've made and seek a better life. One that doesn't make me close my eyes to the richness around me in favour of the riches money can buy. I want that life you spoke of Molly. The family, the love and the commitment. I want to laugh and be happy and take pleasure in the small things. The smile of a loved one and a fabulous sunset. The scent of a rose and the smell of baking bread. I want to hear my child's laughter and watch them grow and I want to meet a man who loves me and shares my dreams. When I walked into Bluebell cottage, I saw that was possible. It has a magic that surrounds it that took my breath away. You say this isn't my fight but you're wrong. This is my greatest battle because I'm fighting for my future."

Molly smiles and reaches out and grasps my hand, squeezing it tightly. Then she reaches for Jack's and her eyes sparkle. "I hope it works out for you all. One thing I believe in is fate. You need to reach deep inside yourselves and make it happen. If there's a way, you will find it and if it's meant to be, then it will happen."

The silence between us speaks volumes. We are all struggling to understand how we can make a difference and then Jack says, "You know, you could help us, Molly."

She shakes her head. "I doubt that, Jack but tell me anyway."

He looks excited. "Don't sell to them. Tell them Bluebell cottage is not for sale and we will try to work out a way to buy it from you ourselves."

I gaze at him sharply and see that he means every word. Sally looks confused. "How can we do that, Jack? Bluebell cottage will be more money than we can raise between us?"

I say slowly, "I may have an idea."

They look across and I say with determination.

"I think I have a way but it will need a couple of things agreed before I can proceed. Leave it with me and I'll raise the money."

They look surprised but then Molly shakes her head. "I'm sorry, dear, even if you raise the money, you're too late."

I feel a dart of apprehension hit me as she says sadly, "Bluebell cottage has already been sold."

♥22

The ride home was a silent one. When Molly told us Bluebell cottage was sold, I felt all hope leave us. I stare out of the window and wish I could dissolve into tears right here. This is all too much. Molly assured us it was in the hands of the same property company that owned Honeysuckle cottage. That did little to reassure us. All that means is they have a bigger investment to realise when the consortium comes calling.

Sally is the first to speak. "I'm sorry, Rachel. You meant well but what can we do now? Even if we do raise the money, it could be futile because the land may still be sold. Our cottages occupy the best views and Bert and Sheila will be no match for the sharks that operate in the sea of big business. Maybe we should just accept this and move on."

Jack nods despondently and I face them angrily. "Absolutely not. So what if she's sold Bluebell cottage? The first thing to do is for you to give me the name of the management company you rent Honeysuckle cottage from. I'll do some digging and see if we can salvage something from this. Secondly, we go ahead with the fundraiser. With Logan's offer, it's achievable. Thirdly, I need something from you Sally that I'm not sure you'll want to reveal and then I must do something I've been dreading since the moment I got here."

Jack says sharply, "Which is?"

I sigh heavily. "Go home."

For the rest of the journey, I outline my plans. We soon reach home and Sally heads back to feed Vixen and find what I need. To my surprise she didn't question my strange request just shrugged and nodded her agreement.

Jack walks me to Bluebell cottage and I'm grateful for his support. As we reach the door, he says fearfully, "When will you be leaving?"

Shrugging, I open the door and as he follows me in, I look around with a new determination. "I suppose it needs to be the sooner the better. I can't put off the inevitable, despite how much I want to."

He moves across and we stand shoulder to shoulder staring at the bay that sparkles like a jewel in a turbulent war. He turns to me and I see his eyes soften and stare into my soul and I shift towards him involuntarily as he meets me in the middle. We are almost touching and I think I hold my breath as he reaches down and runs his fingers through my hair.

He says softly, "You are so beautiful, Rachel, both inside and out. I want you to know that I'm going nowhere and any decision you make, I'll support you."

Then he pulls my face to his and our lips touch in the gentlest of ways. It feels like the end of one chapter and the beginning of another and who knows how the story will end? This kiss is the first one of a lifetime's supply. Jack's the man I was always mean to find. Now I just need to make it happen.

As I wave Jack off hours later, I feel warm inside. I can't believe something so amazing has come out of the same day that devastated my new cosy bubble. The best day of my life sits side by side one of the worst and takes the edge off what is about to be an even more difficult task.

Reaching for my phone, I take a deep breath and do what I've been dreading. Turn off the 'do not disturb.'

As expected, the phone starts buzzing angrily. It lights up like a cockpit in an aeroplane and my heart sinks. Notifications start multiplying and the text alert appears on repeat as it comes to life before my eyes. As I watch my phone implode on itself, my life soon follows. What was I thinking taking off like that? It was selfish, foolish and now I'll have to deal with the consequences.

Tentatively, I dial voicemail and my legs start shaking as I listen to them one by one. Most of them are from Spencer who starts off slightly annoyed, then becomes angry and finally worried. There are many from the office with the usual queries and just one from my father asking me to call him as soon as I get the message.

I feel the tears building as I realise, I can't walk away from that life. Why did I ever think I could?

Choosing my father above everybody else, I call him and hold my breath waiting for him to reply.

As I hear his soft voice, I almost crumble – almost.

"Hey, are you ok, honey?"

I gulp and say softly.

"I'm not sure."

He says gently.

"Why didn't you say something?"

"Say what?"

"That it was all becoming too much. We could have dealt with it properly."

I sigh heavily. "I'm sorry, dad. It was a spur-of-the-moment thing and I couldn't see beyond my need for some space. Maybe it's been building for some time but that day was kind of unusual and something happened to make me snap."

He says in his calm, reassuring, voice. "Do you want to tell me about it?"

I sigh heavily. "Not right now. I suppose I should come back and sort this mess out."

There's a brief silence and then he surprises me by saying. "This business has run my life and you know the sacrifices I made to get where we are. I never wanted that for you. I thought it would be easier because most of the hard work had been done. However, we both know that's not the case. When you came into the business, I was the proudest father in the world. My little girl wanting to work side by side with me in the family business. But you were better than me, Rachel. You breathed new life into it and took it further than we ever thought possible. You saw things the rest of us were blind to and you're the person responsible for the success we currently enjoy. No father could be prouder than me at what you've accomplished but I would sacrifice all of that success tomorrow if I thought you were unhappy. I want that above all else, darling and so tell me what I can do to make it right."

A sob escapes as the pressure I'm feeling starts to evaporate. I'm that little girl again who ran to her father when she was upset or hurt. The little girl who sat on her father's knee while he stroked her hair and told her everything would be ok. Why didn't I go to him first and let him deal with things as he's always done? Then I realise I'm not that little girl anymore. I'm an adult and wanted to make him proud. How could I run to him with my problems? He was so happy relinquishing control of his company while he did the things he never could when I was growing up. Finally, he has a life free of business and time to spend with my mother as they enjoy retirement. How could I drag him back to somewhere I wanted to escape from?

He says gently. "You know, whatever's bothering you, take time. Take as much of it as you like. Maybe go on holiday, travel a bit and forget about work. Take Spencer with you and enjoy some time to get to know each other outside of the office. I'll step back in for as long as it takes. I just want you to be happy, Rachel. That's all I've ever wanted."

I gulp and say sadly, "I needed to get away from everything daddy, including and most of all Spencer."

I hear him draw his breath and a hint of steel creeps into his voice.

"What's he done?"

I sniff. "I'd rather not say, just that I needed time to think and now I know he was never the man for me. I've found a place I belong, dad. A place where nobody knows who I am and what I do. They accept me for me, Rachel Asquith. A lost and lonely girl who came here with nothing. They have taken me in and made me part of their lives. I'm happy here but I know I must resolve things in London."

There's a slight pause, and he says softly, "Are you saying you want out completely? Start again somewhere else and leave this all behind?

The tears fall thick and fast, as I whisper, "I'm not sure. All I know is I'm happy for the first time in years. It's made me realise what's important and

I want to grab it hard and hold on to it for as long as possible."

He says softly, "And Spencer? What about him?"

Sighing heavily, I chew my lip as I voice the words I've known for some time. "It's over. I need to come back and end it properly. Don't get me wrong, Spencer's an amazing CEO, one of the best and excellent at his job. The trouble is, he's not the man I want anymore. Our relationship is built on an ideal. There is no substance to it and I want the fairy tale."

To my surprise, my father laughs softly. "That's my girl. You always did believe in fairy tales and now you must set yourself free to find yours. Come home, Rachel and do what you must but know that whatever you decide I'll support you all the way."

The love I have for my father at this moment threatens to crush me. I couldn't love him any more than I do and it gives me the courage to face the past. So, I take a deep breath and say softly, "I'll catch the train in the morning. I'll head to the apartment first and then the office. Will you be there?"

"If you want me to be."

"Of course, I want you there. Just let me sort things out with Spencer first in my own way. Anyway, I should call him, I can't put this off any longer."

As I make to end the call, I say softly, "I love you, daddy, and… thank you."

He says gruffly, "I love you too, sweetheart. Have a safe journey and I'll see you tomorrow."

He hangs up and I stare at the phone that has made possible the conversation I was hoping to hear. The love I have for my father… my family, was never in question. Now I just need to repair the damage in my personal life.

As I lift the phone to make the call, I dread the most, I'm emotionally exhausted. I can't face the questions that are sure to spill from Spencer's angry lips, so I take the cowards way out. Instead, I text him a short, clipped, message, designed to do the job for me.

Spencer, we need to talk. Meet me in your office tomorrow at 2 pm. I'll explain everything then.

I don't care that it was short and to the point. I'm an emotional wreck after the conversation with my father and can't think straight. Now is not the best time to deal with Spencer Scott so, I put off the inevitable confrontation until I have time to gather my courage and strength.

As I lie in bed with the moon shining its light through the window, I think about tomorrow. Whatever it brings will be difficult but there is no other way. My future hangs in the balance and I wonder which way the scales will fall.

Sleep does not come easily tonight as I think of what lies ahead.

♥23

The next morning, I am up before the sun. Sleep was not kind to me last night and I am keen to get this day over with. As I pack a small bag to take with me, I feel sad as I contemplate leaving this all behind. The train's not for a few hours so I wander outside and decide to take an early morning walk to distract my attention.

The air is crisp and clear and I walk slowly along the cliffs watching the waves crashing to the shore below. The sound is comforting and yet invigorating. Nature at its most raw and as I look out across the ocean, all I see is emptiness. The sun has yet to wake and I feel the chill of the early morning.

Wrapping my arms around my body, I hug myself to keep warm. It's just me and mother nature working out a way forward until I'm aware of a figure jogging along the cliff path towards me. Looking up, my heart sinks as I see Logan obviously out for an early morning jog. Great, just what I need, today of all days.

As I watch him approach, I can't deny it's a spectacular sight. He must have been running for a while because his shirt is soaked and he looks as if he's been up for some time. He sees me in his path and slows down and jogs towards me. "Well, well, my accident-prone neighbour. What's the matter, couldn't you sleep?"

I roll my eyes and throw him my most disdainful look.

"Actually, I'm an early riser and always think nature's at its finest in the early hours. I like the solitude it offers and the peace and quiet to contemplate the day ahead."

He laughs softly which for some reason makes him look almost human. He looks at me for a moment and I watch as his eyes narrow and he says curtly, "What's on your mind?"

Maybe it's because I'm feeling low and in need of a friend right now but my usual sharp retort deserts me and I sigh heavily. "Is it that obvious?"

He surprises me by reaching out and pulling me down beside him on the grass overlooking the bay. Then he places his arm around me and pulls me close, rubbing my shoulder reassuringly. I'm not sure why but this simple act of kindness brings tears to my eyes as I welcome the warmth he gives me both physically and mentally. He says softly, "Like I said, what's the problem?"

Battling to stop the tears from giving away how vulnerable I am right now, I say sadly, "I must go back to London. We went to see Molly yesterday, and she told us that Bluebell cottage was already sold to the development company that owns

Honeysuckle cottage. If we are to stand any chance of fighting the developers, I need to return to London and use every inch of my power to help."

Logan says softly, "And you have to face what you left behind."

I nod. "Yes, there's a lot of unfinished business that needs sorting. The one I'm dreading the most is my relationship. I know he cheated on me but it's a lot to face. Spencer wasn't just my fiancé, he's the CEO of Viking foods. He will never go away and it'll be messy."

Logan rubs my shoulder and says firmly, "What if you left and did what you came here for, start again?"

I lay my head on his shoulder and say sadly, "I can't. I thought I could but there's something you don't know."

He says nothing and just keeps on rubbing my shoulder giving me the courage to speak.

"I *am* Viking foods, Logan. It's my father's company that he started many years ago. It always did well but when I came into the business it thrived. I was lucky, I guess. I hit on a product that's at the forefront of everyone's minds. My Vegan ready meal range sells out wherever it goes. Distribution is high and the demand even higher. We had to increase production, but it's still not enough. We just can't make it fast enough and the business is exploding. That was my brainchild and

I'm required to see this through. More and more opportunities are being presented to us and it's difficult to keep up with them. If I walk away, yes things would continue but Viking foods is my inheritance. If I go, my father will step back in charge and I'm not prepared to take his retirement away from him."

Logan says nothing just carries on rubbing my shoulder and I'm ashamed to admit I like it. I like the fact he's here and a friendly ear to listen to my worries. I feel as if a huge burden has lifted and am grateful that he doesn't throw any cutting remarks or cracks any jokes at my expense.

Sighing, I look at the ocean and say sadly, "I wish things were different. I want all of this, the life I thought I'd have. A loving husband, a couple of kids and a nice house. No worries and time to enjoy life and not have to think about deadlines and problems. When I came here, I saw that life. The people here are genuine and don't judge. There's a simplicity to it that frees my mind and now that's all under threat because once again, big business just can't stop manipulating life for a profit."

Logan drops his arm and pulls my face to his. I see him looking at me with a fierce determination that takes my breath away.

"Listen to yourself, you're giving up in your mind already. I always had you down as a fighter and you know what needs to be done here. There's a reason you came to Perivale, and that's because it needs someone like you to hold its hand through a crisis. Well, I am going to return the favour. Go and make yourself ready to do battle and I'll be right there by your side. I'll come with you to London and provide you the back-up you need - if you need it."

I stare at him in shock. "What! You would come to London just to back me up… why?"

He grins. "Because I can and I need to go and sort some business out there, anyway. You do what you need to and if you need a friendly face, just call me and I'll come running."

I laugh softly, "You'll come jogging you mean."

He laughs, then pulls me up, saying, "Now go. I'll pick you up in an hour and we'll use the journey to work out a plan of action."

He turns and starts jogging back the way he came before I can raise any objections. I'm not sure why but I'm glad he was here. Logan Rivers is probably just what I need right now. A formidable friend to keep me from folding. Could this place really get any better than it is?

♥24

The train journey was interesting. Logan didn't give me any time to dwell on my subsequent meeting with Spencer and just helped me talk over what I needed to do. I told him of my idea to help raise the money and he was full of helpful advice.

By the time the train pulls into London Bridge station my head is clearer and I feel more like the person I was before that fateful day.

Logan leaves me to take a taxi to my apartment and says firmly, "Call me if you need me. I'll be in meetings but will come as quickly as I can. You're not on your own here and even if it's just a word of advice or someone to blow off steam to, I'm your man."

He winks as he holds open the door of the taxi for me and a part of me wishes he would jump in after me. Having him here has taken the edge off my return and I smile at him with appreciation and say meaningfully, "Thank you for being here when I needed you."

Just for a second, his eyes soften and the look he sends me gives me chills. Then he says softly, "I always am, Rachel. Now, go and cause havoc, I know you're good at that."

Grinning, I slam the door closed and instruct the driver where to take me.

As I settle back in the seat, I can't stop smiling.

It feels strange coming home. The familiar streets and buildings I see every day look somehow different now. I notice the dust on the streets and the rubbish spilling from the bins. People walk by without a glance and bird song has been replaced by traffic. The building I call home looks impersonal and disdainful. Modern, sleek, cold and unwelcoming. Just for a moment, I stand to look up at the place I call home and realise my heart moved out of here months ago.

The ride in the elevator gives me time to still my beating heart. How will I feel when I place that key in the lock? Will Spencer be waiting, or will he stay true to type and be firmly seated at his office desk? Did Camilla come here and have they shared more than just a fancy meal in the time I've been away?

Shaking my head, I can't believe it's only been just over a week. It feels like a lifetime ago. So much has happened and most of it good, actually no, most of it great. I've met a strong group of friends and I've met... Jack.

Thinking of Jack always brings a smile to my lips and causes my heart to flutter. He is everything I thought I'd never find and everything I hoped for. He is kind, thoughtful and so sexy it makes me shiver with excitement. Thinking about Jack in London makes me laugh. He would be like a fish out of water. He would hate this place and I can't see him ever wanting to come here. No, Jack is a village lad, and it suits him.

Logan, on the other hand, well, I *can* imagine him in London. He is just the sort of man who would stare at it with a challenge in his eye. We are a lot alike and yet there's something about him that confuses me. One minute I hate him and the next he surprises me by showing a softer side that he keeps well hidden. There's also a lot of sexual tension between us and not for the first time, I wonder what it would be like to feel his lips on mine and that amazing body pressed hard against my own.

Feeling suddenly hot, I'm glad when the lift stops and I start the familiar walk towards apartment 215. The home I share with Spencer.

I'm almost afraid to venture inside but when I do, I'm surprised to find I feel nothing. There's a detachment in me that makes me look around critically. Everything looks the same but different somehow.

Walking around, I see the epitome of chic sophistication. Chrome and mirrors, much like in Logan's beach house but without the comfort. Every conceivable gadget with Spencer's pride and joy hanging on the wall - a 75" TV screen that he had flown in specially. The kitchen is spotless which merely shows it's never used. We eat out a lot or just heat up ready meals. This is a place to rest our heads after a busy day, not a home filled with light and warmth. We rarely entertain and never just relax cooking together after a hard day's work.

Usually, we are both so wrapped up in work we carry it on when we get home. Any intimacies we share are reserved for bedtime before the lights go out. Even that has been fewer than normal as our demanding days sap our energy making sleep the only thing we crave.

I look at the panoramic view of London and sigh inside. We were so busy building our future we forgot to weave love into the bricks. There are no hopes and dreams making up the cement, and we just kept on going until we reached the top. Maybe that's why it's all about to come crumbling down around our feet now.

Sighing, I head to our bedroom and prepare to make myself into the hard-edged business woman I need right now. When I face Spencer and the staff at Viking foods, it will be as their Chairman and nothing else.

Now I know why it's called power dressing. I feel like superwoman. A black pencil skirt and fitted jacket over a white blouse give me the edge I need. My stiletto's make me walk taller and the band pulling my hair back severely reminds me I have a job to do. I hide behind a full face of make-up and clutch my briefcase with authority. I'm back and not about to be messed around. Too much depends on it.

A short Tube ride to the office gives me enough time to steel my resolve. The girl in me has been left behind in Perivale while the woman I am takes charge.

As I stride into the reception of my own building, I see the looks reserved for the boss. Me.

Angela the receptionist looks up in surprise. Miss Asquith, it's good to see you.

I nod. "You too, Angela. I hope the family are well?"

She nods and smiles as I head towards the waiting elevator. A few people share my journey but none of them speak. Many people work for Viking foods and I'm ashamed to admit I know only a handful of names. A brief nod or smile to the more familiar ones is all they get, and they would rather be anywhere else but seen talking to me.

That's fine, I get it. The boss's daughter became their boss and is definitely not one of them. *I* would distance myself from a person like me, it's normal. So, I just nod as expected and walk purposefully towards Spencer's office, ignoring the curious looks as I pass. Then, as I reach my destination, I take a deep breath and step inside.

He looks up and our eyes meet across the familiar room. Spencer Scott is an impressive man. He wears his status well and always looks immaculate in a tailored suit and silk tie. His hair is styled by the finest barber and his manicured hands tell of a man who does no physical work. Despite everything, I am actually pleased to see him.

He looks at me with reserve, I've confused him and he doesn't know what he's facing. I don't miss the relief in his eyes though as he says softly, "It's good to see you, Rachel."

I smile briefly as I approach his desk which he vacates to meet me halfway. Tentatively, he reaches out and I allow myself to be drawn into his embrace. Spencer feels familiar. The constant in my life that has grown over years of working so closely together. He is the only person I have seen every day for the last few years and nothing can change the fondness I feel for him.

Just for a moment, we stand together like we always have. He holds me gently and I take comfort from him as I've always done. This time though, I feel the difference. Nothing has really changed between us, I can see that now. We were always these people standing here and should never have tried to be anything other than good friends.

He pulls back and smiles softly, reaching for my hair. "Suits you."

I shrug. "I fancied a change."

"Obviously."

He drops my hand and says with a slight edge to his voice.

"Are you going to tell me what this is all about?"

Sighing, I sit on the couch in his office and pat the seat beside me. "Of course, you deserve that at least."

He perches on the edge of the seat and just for a moment words desert me. I'm not sure where to begin but then he says, "Where have you been?"

A simple question that deserves an answer and I sigh heavily.

"On a journey, Spencer. A life-changing journey that started the day I ditched a meeting in favour of getting my hair done."

He raises his eyes and I laugh softly. "As it happens, it altered a lot more than my appearance. I decided to skip the meeting you had planned and do something wild for once. I found myself in front of a hairdresser not far from here and thought that was all I'd be explaining. However, I sat next to a woman who got my attention in more ways than one."

He looks at me curiously but even now he doesn't add up the pieces. Fixing him with a hard look, I say bitterly, "Does the name Camilla ring any bells?"

Suddenly, the penny drops and I see the panic enter his eyes. At first, I think he's going to deny all knowledge of her but he must see the resolve in my face and slumps beside me looking guilty as charged.

"I'm sorry, Rachel."

I breathe out and realise I'd been holding my breath. I'm not sure why but I don't even feel angry anymore. He looks at me with a pained expression and says guiltily. "I'm not sure why I cheated on you? There was no reason other than the excitement. Camilla was someone who just happened to be there."

I raise my eyes. "What on Tinder where you met? It's funny, Spencer but I may have missed the part where people who are living with another, oh and engaged to that same person, start advertising for a partner on Tinder."

He looks contrite but I shake my head.

"Something she said in that hairdressers hit me where it hurt and I'm not talking about the fact she thought you were going to propose."

He looks shocked and I laugh softly. "I take it you didn't, at least, not a marriage one."

He continues to look uncomfortable and I say sadly. "She told me you said you needed a wife to distract you from business. That hurt because even then I tended to agree with her."

Taking his hand in mine, I say gently. "We fell into this relationship because it's what we both wanted. We got on well and the physical attraction was there, so it was inevitable. The trouble is, we worked too closely together and there was no room to grow. You were right in what you said, you need somebody to make you forget about work when you're not here, and so do I. We took our work home with us and there was no room for anything else. We were more like flatmates and so, of course, it was doomed to fail."

Spencer shakes his head. "It may have ended up that way, but I fell in love with you, Rachel. Who wouldn't? Maybe you're right and we should have remained friends but I don't regret a minute of our time together."

We share a smile and I know I could never hate Spencer. What happened was written in the stars and was the wake-up call we both needed.

Sighing, I shake my head and smile shakily. "I suppose what I'm saying, is we can no longer be in a personal relationship but I still want us to be friends and colleagues. You're good at your job and we make a great team in the boardroom and just confused that with the bedroom."

Sadly, I remove my engagement ring and hold it out to him. "Make sure the next woman who receives a ring from you is the one, Spencer. The woman who completes you and someone you look forward to spending time with. Make sure you choose well because it's probably the most important decision you will ever make."

Spencer looks emotional as he takes the ring from my hands and says sadly, "I never meant for it to end this way, Rachel. If it means anything, I'm sorry. I did love you, hell, I still do, but you're right as always. We should just be the best of friends with no benefits."

He smiles and I laugh softly feeling as if a huge weight has lifted.

Then he says with interest, "So are you going to tell me where you've been?"

I smile. "I've been to Hell which led me to paradise. Now I just have to work out a way to save it from destruction."

He looks confused and I smile feeling a little like my old self.

"I need your help though. Meet me in the boardroom in half an hour. I have a plan that may make a lot of people extremely happy."

♥25

The first person I see when I reach the Boardroom is my father. He holds out his arms and I fall into them as I've always done. He strokes my hair lovingly and whispers, "Welcome home, sweetheart."

Squeezing my eyes tightly shut, I try not to let the emotion take hold. I need a clear head now and won't let Perivale down.

We pull apart as Spencer arrives and I don't miss the frosty look my father gives him. Smiling at him reassuringly I say to my father, "You may as well know that Spencer and I have agreed to call off the engagement. There are no hard feelings and we remain firm friends."

Spencer smiles ruefully and I see the emotion in his eyes as my father sighs. "I'm sorry, guys. I know it must have taken a lot to admit things weren't right. You did the right thing though and you both have my full support."

He looks to me and says firmly, "Now, Rachel. Tell us your idea and then we can work out what can be done about it."

As I fill them in on everything, to their credit, they don't interrupt. Spencer takes notes and my father looks thoughtful.

When I finish, he recaps. "So, you want us to manufacture a new line with the profits going to restore the village hall in Perivale. How does this make good business sense?"

Spencer nods and I smile knowingly. "Because it will be the best publicity for our new range. Quite honestly these cakes of Sally's are the best I've ever tasted. She has this magical combination of ingredients that somehow work so well together, nobody would ever guess what they were. One taste is all it would take and the publicity would create a snowball effect across the country. Sally's, cake sale stands to benefit every good cause that takes it on and provides us with a very healthy bottom line. We create a publicity campaign that would help any fundraiser in the country. We would sell them initially as a package including promotional material to promote their good cause. Any profits raised would be donated to the cause with a special mention on our website. Once the public taste them demand will be high, so we will gain contracts with every supermarket chain in the country. I visualise prime positions in stores and a marketing campaign that would elevate Sally's cakes to the top."

My father sits back as Spencer says softly, "This could take months of planning. The production schedule is already operating at full capacity. How can we factor this in?"

I smile at him with a confidence I don't feel. "That's why I need you, Spencer. I've never met a man who could pull this out of the bag like you could. This is what you love. You want a challenge to get your teeth into and you must see the potential in this. I propose we start the hype immediately with the first packs going out in just 4 weeks' time. The place we launch the campaign is Perivale village hall where we will invite the press and supermarket buyers to taste the product. The national exposure will highlight the problem that Perivale faces and turn the spotlight on the hotel project and the destruction of an area of outstanding beauty. Viking foods will appear to be the one saving the environment and it will tie up nicely with our vegan campaign."

Spencer smiles with admiration and turns to my father. "You know, I think this may just work. I'll get onto it right away and see if I can run a few costings and call in a few favours."

My father nods and says firmly, "Make it happen, Spencer. Rachel's right, this is an opportunity that we can't ignore and if it puts a smile on my daughters face, it will be worth every hour we spend on making it happen."

Spencer nods and I look around gratefully. "Thank you, guys. I really mean that. I wasn't sure how I'd feel coming back. So much has happened and my outlook has changed dramatically. However, being here with you both and on familiar territory, I must say, feels good."

Spencer says softly, "So what next for Rachel?"

My father looks at me keenly and I sit back and say slowly, "I'm just working that part out. I'm thinking I may just need to phone a friend for their advice."

♥26

I meet up with Logan at a restaurant in Knightsbridge that's always been a firm favourite of mine. When I see him waiting for me it feels good to see him. He doesn't look out of place among the well-heeled diners and judging by the number of admiring stares he gathers as he moves across to greet me, I'd say he was where he belongs.

He reaches me and smiles, "Well… how did it go?"

The broad smile on my face must say it all because his face softens, and he says, "It went well then."

I nod as I take my seat and watch as he sits across from me. As I fill him in on what happened, I see the admiration grow in his eyes. By the time I've finished, he nods with appreciation. "You've done well. I always knew you would come to the right conclusion."

Leaning back in my seat, I say with confusion. "But how can I have both, Logan? I want the life in Perivale but I can't ignore the excitement I felt when I was back in my business. How is it possible to have both?"

He looks at me thoughtfully. "Anything's possible if you want it badly enough."

The way he says it makes me stop and stare. His voice had a softness to it that spoke beyond the meaning of his words. The intense look he gives me makes me struggle to breathe and I can't tear my eyes away. I try to regain my composure and picture Jack waiting in Perivale for me to return. Jack's the man I want, of course, he is but right now he seems like a dream.

Shaking the image away, I try to focus on my problem. "I told my father I was heading back to Perivale tomorrow. I promised to take my laptop and work from Bluebell cottage to make this happen. The trouble is, there's no internet connection so I may have to arrange for one. That may take a little time, so I was hoping to ask any of the neighbours if I could use theirs."

Logan says in a firm voice. "You can use my home as your office. I won't disturb you because I have business of my own to attend to."

I look at him with interest. "Of course, you came here for a reason too. How did that go?"

He winks as he takes a sip of his wine. "Very well. I have a buyer for the new game who has promised the £50,000 donation to the village hall fund. I need to iron out a few bugs and then it can go into production. I'm anticipating it should be ready in approximately six weeks."

I raise my glass in a toast. "To big business and using it for good."

Logan clinks my glass with his and says, "To Perivale and its future."

We share a smile over a job well done. Now we just need to head home with the good news.

♥

When we arrive back it feels as if I'm home. We share a taxi from the station and as it stops outside Bluebell cottage, I stare at the pretty house and smile happily.

Logan says softly, "How does it feel to be back?"

I say wistfully, "Like I've come home."

We head inside and the little cottage welcomes me back like an old friend and I feel calm and content.

Logan looks around and smiles before saying loudly, "I'll leave you to it. I'll catch you later."

As he turns to leave, I say loudly, "Thank you."

He smiles. "For what?"

"For being the best friend, a girl could wish for."

I don't miss the disappointment in his eyes as he smiles tightly. "Of course, I'll see you soon, Rachel. Try to stay out of trouble, if that's at all possible."

My laughter follows him out and I look around me happily. This is where my heart now lives. Now I just have to work out a way to have it all.

♥27

Waking up in Bluebell cottage the next morning is different somehow. A huge weight has lifted and I stretch out happily as I hear the birds singing outside. Thinking back to yesterday, I smile to myself. Spencer surprised me. I never thought he would be so understanding and yet when I confronted him, he almost looked relieved. Sadly, I realise he must have felt as trapped as I did. Maybe he had second thoughts a long time ago, and the dalliances were a result of that. I'm glad we're still friends though. It would have been messy if he'd taken it badly.

With a new spring in my step, I get ready for the day ahead. I can't wait to share my news with the others and so make short work of getting washed and dressed and am soon venturing outside into the glorious sunshine.

Heading over to Sally's, I hope she's in because of everyone she deserves to hear this first.

She answers the door in a bright orange jumpsuit with her hair dyed black. She looks almost normal, albeit like an inmate from an American penitentiary. She smiles as she sees me waiting and beckons me inside.

"Morning, Rachel, or is it afternoon? I've been up so long now I'm not sure if it's even the same day anymore."

Laughing, I shake my head. "Why, what have you been doing?"

She smiles and leads me to her art room. "I wanted to paint an order I've been sitting on for some time."

As I look at the painting nestling on the canvas, it takes my breath away. She has painted the most fabulous sunset over a dark, raging sea. The colours are vibrant and I can almost see the waves crashing angrily to shore and look at her in amazement. "This is seriously good, Sally."

She shrugs. "If you say so. It's for a customer who lives abroad most of the year. This is the view from their apartment and the guy wanted it as a wedding present for his wife."

"Well, you've certainly done an amazing job. Um… do you always dress like your paintings though?"

Looking down, Sally laughs. "A lot of the time I do. I'm not sure why, I suppose the colours are in my mind and I dress accordingly. Maybe subconsciously it gets me in the right frame of mind. Weird, huh?"

We laugh and I look at her fondly. "There's nothing weird about you, Sally."

We head towards her kitchen and she makes me a mug of her strange herbal tea, saying apologetically. "Sorry, the cake all went yesterday. Max came by and cleaned me out."

Fighting back the disappointment, I say with interest, "How is the incorrigible Max?"

She smiles. The same mad Max he's always been. I had to throw him out in the end because he was hanging around when I needed to get on. I'm heading up to meet him for lunch though, would you like to come?"

I laugh softly. "Do you think he'd mind?"

She looks surprised. "Of course not, the more the merrier. Max loves a crowd."

She takes a sip of her tea and I watch her carefully. I wonder what she would think if Max made his move? Sally appears blind to what is obvious to everyone else. Max is crazy about her and I'm not sure if she feels the same.

I fill her in on what happened in London and she looks surprised. "They actually went for it. I can't believe it. Why would anyone want my cakes?"

I shake my head in amazement. "The whole world would want your cakes if they tasted them, Sally. Even if they hate cake normally, they would be converted. I'm not sure you know how good they really are."

She shrugs. "I don't care, really. I make them because I enjoy it and if they can help raise money for good causes, then I'm happy with that."

Picking my words carefully, I say seriously, "You know, we are prepared to pay you a hefty percentage for your recipe. It's how business works. It will be your name we use unless you prefer otherwise and your recipes. You stand to earn a lot of money from this along with the good causes. I'm not sure you realise that."

She shakes her head. "I never thought about the money, Rachel. I'm just happy to help. Wouldn't it make more sense to just give more to the good causes? My art pays me, not my hobby."

I say firmly, "We will pay you properly otherwise we would be doing something unethical. What you then choose to do with the money is up to you. You can give it all away or use it to secure your future. Maybe I should put you in touch with a financial advisor. They will outline your options."

Sally looks horrified. "Oh, please don't, Rachel. I couldn't think of anything worse than discussing money. I'd rather not thanks."

As she refills the mugs, I vow to make sure Sally gets everything she deserves. Changing the subject, I ask about Jack.

She looks at me with a troubled look and immediately I tense up. "Um… yes, he's fine. I saw him yesterday when you were away. He popped by with um… Fiona. She's back for a while and they spent some time catching up."

She looks at me anxiously and I try every trick in the book not to look affected. However, inside my stomach is tying itself up in knots as I say in a slightly high voice. "Oh… that's nice. Um… is she staying long?"

Sally shrugs. "I'm not sure, they didn't say. They were taking Millie for a walk on the cliffs and stopped by to say hi."

I smile weakly. "That's nice."

Suddenly, the sun has lost its shine and the bird song sounds as if they're mocking me. The day has lost its sparkle and I feel a sense of something shifting in my perfect life. Sally must see how the news has affected me and says softly, "We should head over to Bert and Sheila's. They are anxious to hear how things went in London."

Nodding, I follow her, trying to erase the picture of Jack with his ex-girlfriend from my mind.

♥

Bert and Sheila appear quite tense and I feel bad. They're obviously worrying about the situation and look at me anxiously as I head inside with Sally. Sheila says with relief, "Rachel, thank goodness you're back. We had a most unwelcome visit from Christopher Masters yesterday and I'm still shaking from it."

I look at them with alarm. "Why, what did he say?"

Bert says gloomily. "Came here unannounced and tried to charm his way in. He made a big show of pointing out the failings of living in such an isolated spot and offered us a large sum of money to move somewhere more suitable, as he put it."

Sheila narrow her lips. "Well, I told him what he could do with his offer. Sent him away with a flea in his ear and left him in no doubt as to what I'd do to him if he ever showed up here again."

I smile at the picture of Christopher Masters getting a dressing down from Sheila and say softly, "You know he won't give up. I expect he'll increase his offer until you give in. Money has a habit of doing that for people."

Bert shakes his head. "We don't need his money, everything we need is here. No, it spurred us into action and we haven't been idle."

Sheila rolls her eyes. "Don't get your hopes up. Bert has decided to form an action group named, Protect Perivale."

He looks pleased with himself. "Yes, I've enrolled in The Facebook and am in the process of setting up my page as they call it. Are you on the Facebook, Sally?"

Sally shakes her head. "Yes, I have a business page on there. I'll like yours if you want me to."

Bert looks pleased. "Well, it needs setting up but hopefully you will like what I've done."

Sally giggles. "It means, I'll like your page. That way I'll see all your posts."

Bert looks confused. "How can you like it before I've made it? Do you receive mail then?"

I share a look with Sally as Sheila nods. "Yes, it's all a bit strange this internet world. Tell them about that man that keeps cropping up, Bert."

Bert nods. "Yes, there are people showing themselves on here that I'm sure I must have known in the past. They want to be my friend which is a bit weird, really. I'm sure they don't live around here although I do believe I've seen one of them in the pub."

Sheila nods. "Yes, I thought I recognised him from there. It's funny how they know we're there, I wonder if they've heard it from somewhere."

Sally giggles and I say patiently, "It's just Facebook suggesting people you may know. They throw them up based on your location and the information you provide. It's a bit spooky, really."

Bert looks worried and Sheila says, "How do they know? I told Bert this was a bad idea, didn't I Bert? You hear of all sorts. Tape a bit of tissue to that camera, Bert. They are probably watching us right now and listening in on our conversation. You hear terrible things of the internet, girls. I'm not sure we're safe really in our own homes. The

Facebook may not be the best option, Bert. Maybe we should just deliver leaflets like I suggested."

We giggle and I say softly, "I wouldn't worry, Sheila. It's all done by algorithms and stuff. There is no human watching you through your camera and it's perfectly safe."

Bert looks confused and shakes his head. "I'm too old for this. Maybe we should leave it to you girls to get the word out."

Moving across to sit beside him, I pull the laptop to me. "I'll set it up, don't worry. Then I'll show you how it all works. It's actually a wonderful tool for engaging with people you lost touch with years ago. Don't be afraid of what you don't understand. Just make sure you learn and I'm guessing you'll love it when you see what it can do."

They look at me gratefully as Sally jumps up.

"I'll be getting back. Why don't you all come to Max's for lunch? I told him I'd be there at 1 o'clock. We could walk together."

As she heads out, I concentrate on the task in hand of bringing Bert and Sheila kicking and screaming into the digital age.

♥28

It takes the morning to create the 'Save Perivale' action group and I think Bert and Sheila are more confused than ever before we break for lunch. We did manage to connect them with some friends of theirs and they enjoyed seeing their photos and learning what they've been up to.

When Sally calls, I close the laptop and say with some relief. "I'll pop by tomorrow and we'll carry on then. Come on, I don't know about you but I'm so hungry I'll eat anything in my path."

We chat about the problems facing us all the way and by the time we reach Bayside Manor we have run through every possible scenario and are feeling quite despondent.

Max is outside washing his car and watches our approach with a smile.

"Hey, guys it's good to see you. This is unexpected but great at the same time."

He looks at Sally and rolls his eyes. "You're looking orange today, babe, have you been on the sunbed too long?"

She rolls her eyes. "Sorry it's not red, but it's close at least."

Max throws down his cloth and heads across and swings her up in his arms, laughing, "You always brighten my day, babe. Let me feed you up, I can't think of my starving artist locked away all day without any food. You can't just live on cake you know."

Sally laughs as Max carries her into the house. Sharing a knowing look with Sheila we follow them inside.

Max is on fine form today and makes us laugh with tales of life in the Red Arrows. However, the conversation soon turns to the future of Perivale and I fill them in on what happened in London.

Max looks at Sally and smiles proudly. "Look at you, not only are you a talented artist but a super chef too. Is there no end to your talents?"

Sally blushes and Max grins, ruffling her hair playfully. Bert says with concern, "Do you think it will be enough though? I mean, these men don't mess around. We are no match for them."

I look at him thoughtfully. "Ordinarily no, but we have something on our side they aren't counting on."

They all turn to me as Max says, "What's that?"

I grin. "Publicity. Once we get the word out Perivale will be known around the country. The cake sale in its honour will be mirrored in every village hall around the country and every charitable event going. Viking foods will push this and make it a household name and shine the spotlight on our little piece of paradise. If Max manages to get the Red Arrows involved, it will draw the crowds. Logan's games sponsorship will provide a hefty sum to get the work started and the money raised from Sally's Artwork and cake sales means we should soon have enough to remodel the village hall. Therefore, with all our best efforts, it will no longer be a bargaining chip for the planning permission."

Sheila looks confused. "But what if the land management company sell your cottages? They could still build their hotel and squeeze us and Max out. I mean, who wants to live on a building site and then with thousands of tourists throughout the year."

I shrug. "I've asked my father to look into the company who bought the cottages. He intends on finding them and offer to buy the properties from them by outbidding any other offer from the consortium. I know it's a gamble because, for all we know, they may have already struck a deal."

Sally looks upset. "I hope not. Where would we go if they terminated our lease?"

Max puts his arm around her reassuringly. "You could move into Bayside Manor. It's empty most of the time, anyway. You both could. We would all be flatmates and you would both be known locally as my harem."

Bert looks excited as Sheila rolls her eyes. "In your dreams, Max."

He winks suggestively, "I didn't know you saw into my dreams, Sheila. Careful, you may find yourself in there."

Sheila blushes and giggles and this time Bert rolls his eyes. "More like your nightmares."

Max turns to Sally and says with interest, "Have you sorted out the paintings you want to sell for the village hall?"

She nods. "Yes, I put them on my website last night. I wasn't really sure how much to ask because they won't mean anything to anyone but me."

Sheila says with interest, "How much did you ask for?"

Sally shrugs. "Five thousand each. I know it's not a patch on Logan's donation but it should help get some building supplies."

Max looks a little shocked and I shake my head. "Sally, out of everyone you will be raising the most. Add that to your cake money and you will practically be building it yourself."

She shrugs. "Maybe, but I don't see it like that."

Sheila shakes her head. "Well, it sounds as if you've got most things covered. What with Bert's action group on The Facebook and all of your efforts, I think we're doing as much as we can."

Max raises his eyes. "*The* Facebook, what are you talking about?"

Sally giggles. "I'll fill you in later. Anyway, I should get back to my painting."

We stand to leave and I notice Max pull Sally back and hear him say softly, "Will you come and stay tonight, babe? I'll cook you something nice. I'm leaving soon and want to make the most of you while I can."

She smiles happily. "Of course, you know I'd love to."

I stifle a smile as I see her smile and walk away, totally oblivious to the longing in Max's eyes. He catches my eye and smiles softly and then turns away with a little shrug. It makes me laugh as I think of the two of them. Max is used to women falling at his feet just desperate for his attention and Sally hides herself away trying not to draw any attention to herself. I wonder how this will end?

♥29

Later that evening, there's a knock on the door and I'm surprised to see Jack looking as hot as a man has any right to look.

My heart flutters as he smiles sexily and says softly, "Hi."

I can't stop grinning and say shyly, "Hi."

Opening the door, a little wider I invite him in and feel strangely nervous. I busy myself by making some drinks and try to concentrate as he watches me.

"So, how did it go in London?"

I shrug. "Better than I thought. I've managed to get Viking foods behind the project and we should get loads of publicity. I think we're working on six weeks from now to hold the fundraiser at the village hall."

Jack looks impressed and says thoughtfully, "Do you think that would be too late?"

I raise my eyes. "Not really, I mean, it would be months, or years for that matter, for them to sort this out. They still need to acquire the land and submit the revised planning permission. We could object to their every move and tie this one up indefinitely."

Jack shakes his head. "I never know how these things work. It's all alien to me."

Handing him a mug of tea, I smile. "Here, anyway it's good to see you. What's been happening while I've been away?"

He looks a little guilty which makes my heart thump wildly and I hold my breath.

He smiles ruefully. "Fiona came to see me."

Trying desperately to look unconcerned, I say, "Oh, that's nice."

He nods. "It was good to see her and catch up. To be honest, I wasn't sure how I'd feel seeing her again but it felt good. You know, not awkward or anything. We had a nice day and I think we've put everything that happened behind us."

I nod feeling quite sick for some reason. He smiles sweetly. "What about you, did you see the fool while you were there?"

I laugh softly. "Yes, however, like you, we made our peace and parted as friends. It was good to see him and I can relax knowing things have been dealt with properly."

Jack nods and grins. "Then it appears we are both in the same boat."

"What do you mean?"

He laughs. "In a place to move on without the baggage of the past to bring us down."

The relief I feel must show on my face because he sets the mug down and takes my hand in his. "Maybe we can take this slowly and see where it leads. Not rush into anything and just enjoy spending time together. I don't know about you but I'm in no hurry to jump straight into another relationship. However, I would appreciate some very attractive female company that may turn into something special in the future."

For some reason I feel disappointed. I'm not sure what I wanted to hear. I'm happy that Jack appears single and willing to take this further but something is niggling at the back of my mind and I don't know what. So, I just smile and say softly, "I'd like that, Jack."

He leans towards me and lowers his lips to mine and once again his kiss is soft and gentle and speaks of dreams come true and hopeful beginnings. Pushing away the part of me that wants it all now, I accept that he's right. We shouldn't rush into anything. We need to take this slowly and build our relationship with strong foundations. I rushed into one before and should learn from my past mistakes.

As I kiss Jack, I know this is the right decision. We have a lifetime to move forward, and all the fun will be in the journey.

Jack and I spend the rest of the evening together and decide to walk to the nearest pub. It takes about forty minutes but it seems like five as we chat and discover things we didn't know about one another.

As we walk, Jack holds my hand, and it feels so right. Like it was always meant to be there and I am proud to have him walk beside me.

The pub is busy and we almost have to fight for a seat. Luckily, I spy a couple getting ready to leave and quickly jump in their place while Jack waits patiently to be served at the bar.

I must only have sat there for five minutes before an attractive girl heads across from her group of girlfriends and says politely, "I'm sorry to interrupt but are you Rachel?"

I smile. "Yes, sorry, I don't think we've met."

She sits beside me and says warmly, "I'm Fiona, Jack's ex-girlfriend."

Trying not to look shocked, I smile. "I'm pleased to meet you; I've heard only nice things said about you."

She laughs bitterly. "I doubt that. Listen, I hope you don't feel weird or anything but I just wanted to introduce myself. Jack's a great guy and you'll be very lucky if things work out between you."

I'm not sure what to say and she shakes her head. "You know, Rachel. I was a fool to let him go. I thought he was the one - you know the forever one. The trouble is, I wanted to move things on and he didn't. Maybe it's because he's so laid back and easy-going but he wouldn't take the next step and I did something stupid. Now, I can't go back because Jack values loyalty above everything. You're a lucky girl if you win his heart because I did and trampled all over it. Treat him right, Rachel because he deserves it more than most. Jack's a great guy and deserves the best in life."

Jack chooses that moment to return and looks at Fiona in surprise. "Hey, I never saw you come in."

She smiles. "I'm here with the girls, you know, out on the town and looking for fun."

She stands up and says apologetically, "Listen, I'll leave you in peace, I'd better get back. Have a great evening."

She walks back to her friends and I see a hint of sadness in Jack's eyes as he watches her go which sets me on edge.

Then he says ruefully, "I'm sorry, I didn't know she would be here. Was that awkward for you?"

Trying to laugh it off, I raise my eyes. "I never expected her to be so pretty and well... so nice. You must have made a good couple."

He shakes his head. "We did, but that's in the past now. I have a much more attractive date sitting across from me and I want to find out everything Rachel before the end of the evening."

He slides beside me and places his arm around my shoulders, pulling me against him. Leaning down, he whispers, "I've only got eyes for one woman now and she's sitting beside me."

As he drops a light kiss on the top of my head, it chases the doubts away. I'm so lucky to have found Jack in this perfect place and unlike Fiona, I don't intend on messing this up.

♥30

We soon settle into a routine. Max went back to work and Sally threw herself in trying to clear the backlog of orders she's been sitting on.

Bert and Sheila carried on with the, Protect Perivale Facebook group, and I divide my time between London and Bluebell cottage. I took Logan up on his offer for office space and was surprised to find he's not around much. It appears that every time I work, he's away, or out somewhere. I'm not sure why that bothers me but for some reason it does.

Jack and I have been seeing each other whenever we can and I enjoy his company. We either eat at Bluebell cottage or head into Pembury for the odd meal out. Millie accompanies us wherever we go and I love the times when it's just the three of us walking along the cliffs and exploring the beaches. This is what I imagined my perfect life to be. A man who is sweet and kind and whose company I enjoy. A simple life that requires no effort, just a calm, restful, existence, away from the busy life I have in London.

Usually, I spend a couple of days in London catching up with things and Spencer has really stepped up and been the rock I always knew he was.

He has taken over the endless meetings and is working hard on securing the cake project's success. I spend my time at the office with him and he brings me up to date with everything, reminding me what a great team we make.

However, it's Bluebell cottage that I look forward to spending time in the most. Despite its rough edges and lack of amenities, it has a charm all of its own. This is the first place I have ever really felt content and I thank fate for bringing me here in the first place.

♥

The village hall fundraiser day dawns and I feel excited as I realise that everything we've worked so hard for comes to fruition today. Max arrived late last night with his team which has caused much excitement in the whole area. My father and Spencer are travelling down from London along with Logan's sponsors and every local dignitary we could persuade to come. I've booked the press and invited the buyers from the various large retail outlets that we hope to supply with the cakes. I think even the local television cameras will be there and to say I'm nervous is an understatement.

It doesn't take me long to get ready and I find myself watching the clock while I wait. I'm not sure why but I feel on edge even though I've prepared for every eventuality.

I decide to take a walk to clear my head and for a reason I can't explain; I head towards Logan's beach house. I'm not sure why but I have an overwhelming to see him. Any contact we've had in the last few weeks has been minimal and a little awkward if I'm honest. I'm not sure why but it's bothering me, so I decide to see if he's at home and fancies grabbing some breakfast with me to catch up.

It doesn't take long to reach his house and I knock on the door feeling a little foolish. I wonder what he'll think seeing me here? I'm not even sure he's in and turn to leave, when I notice him jogging back along the beach path. As he sees me waiting, he slows down and walks slowly towards me. My heart sinks a little as I see the irritation on his face.

"What's up, Rachel, did you forget something?"

Shaking my head, I say lightly, "Good to see you too. No, I just wondered if you fancied grabbing some breakfast with me."

He raises his eyes and says gruffly, "What's the matter, have you been let down by your *boyfriend*?"

He says the word sarcastically which really gets my back up. He pushes past me and heads inside and I follow him feeling angry.

I watch him stride over to the fridge and grab a bottle of water and as he stands drinking it, I bristle with anger and snap, "For your information, I thought I'd invite you because I haven't seen much of you lately and fancied a catch-up. God only knows why I thought that would be a good idea? I mean, look at you, you shut yourself away from the rest of us and don't have a social bone in your body. You couldn't even be bothered to offer to help set things up today. Instead, you stride around angrily and if anyone dares to ask you to do anything, this is what they get. I'm not sure why I bothered."

He turns and looks at me angrily. "And why do you think I've kept away, Rachel?"

I stare at him in surprise. "How on earth should I know? You're not an easy man to read and quite honestly, I don't know why I keep on trying with you."

I make to leave and he shouts, "Stop right there."

Something in his voice makes me do as he says and as I turn, I see his eyes sparkling with anger. He crosses the room in two strides and grabs my arm and says roughly, "Look at you. You came here chasing the dream you have of the perfect life. You think you've found it but I see things very differently. I've watched you go through the motions doing what you think will get it for you. You stepped out of one relationship into another that's doomed to fail in the same way. You're blind to what is staring at you and has been ever since you arrived and that's what makes me angry, Rachel. You're repeating your past mistakes and just fooling yourself that you've found what you want. That's why I can't stand to be around you because I hate watching you make the same mistake over and over again."

I stare at him in total shock. His eyes are flashing dark and dangerous and he looks so angry I can almost taste it. I'm not sure what to say and his grip on my wrist is starting to hurt. I pull away and say angrily, "How dare you! How bloody dare you speak to me like that! You don't get that right. My choices are my own to make and I'm happy with them."

He laughs bitterly and pushes me until my back is against the wall. Standing before me, he lowers his voice and says huskily, "Does being with Jack set your soul on fire and make you weak inside? Does he light that spark within you that sets off a chain reaction through your body? Is he your first waking thought and the last thing you think of at night? Does he inhabit your dreams and chase the shadows away?"

He runs his fingers down my face gently and whispers, "Does being with him make you lose your mind and does he challenge you in every way? Does he make you feel alive, Rachel or are you just going through the motions? Does his kiss make you lose your mind and do you crave his touch more than air?"

I can feel his hard body against mine and the sweat from his body-skimming my skin, branding it with his scent. He whispers, "When he kisses you, do you feel like the most desirable woman on the planet? Does he hunger for you, Rachel because if the answer is no to any of my questions then he's not the one."

I whisper huskily, "Then who is, Logan?"

His breath fans my face and I lick my lips nervously. I feel my heart beating so loudly he must hear it and my legs are shaking with longing. He says huskily, "Do you want me to kiss you, Rachel?"

The same question again but this time a different answer. I can't help myself as I whisper, "Yes."

His eyes flash dangerously as he holds my head firmly in place. His lips meet mine not in the gentle way that I am accustomed to with Jack. This kiss is raw and potent and invades my soul. Logan enters my mouth like a tornado. He crushes my lips and pulls my body into his. I arch towards him and think I lose my mind as he relentlessly shows me what a proper kiss feels like. I don't see Jack. I don't see Spencer. I don't see anything but Logan. His face fills my mind, body and soul and my heart screams with joy.

He groans which increases my need for him and pulls me closer and savages my lips like an angry animal. I'm left breathless and craving his touch like a drug I need to survive.

Then he pulls away leaving me gasping for air. His breathing is laboured and his eyes sparkle with lust. Then he growls, "You shouldn't settle for anything less than the fairy tale, Rachel."

He turns away and leaves me shaking and fighting to regain some sort of composure.

As my breathing becomes more regular, I think about what I've just done. What *we've* just done and my world stops spinning. Logan is watching me like a wild animal stalking its prey and I stare at him in confusion. He says nothing and yet he says everything with just one look. I think of Jack, Spencer and everything that's happened in the last few weeks and it's too much.

Throwing him an anguished look, I head for the door. He says nothing as I make a hasty exit and run back along the beach to Bluebell cottage. My lips sting from the power of his kiss and my body aches from the effects. So many emotions are invading my mind and body and I can't think straight.

I reach the sanctuary Bluebell cottage offers and throw myself on my bed. I try to block everything out but something is gnawing away at me inside. I wanted Logan so badly. Why does he affect me so deeply? I think back over the weeks. Every meeting, every smart remark and every challenge he threw at me. Then I think of the softer side of him. The little hugs and touches designed for comfort. The listening ear as I poured all my troubles on to his shoulders. The fact he's always there for me with no questions asked and those special times we've shared where we've supported each other when needed.

Then I picture Jack. Kind, soft, caring, Jack. Gentle and sweet and lovely in his own way. Always ready with a smile and good company. He would never let me down and would be a constant companion in my life. The man I always thought I would marry except for one vital thing. There is no spark. No excitement, no conflict, just safety. He isn't the sort to step out of his comfort zone into a world he knows nothing about. He doesn't challenge and carries out everything with a smile. Do I need excitement, do I need that energy that comes with Logan? Groaning, I bury my face in my pillow as my body screams 'yes!' I need a man like Logan because he is compatible with me in every way. He challenges and yet nurtures at the same time. I feel safe with him but there's an edginess to him that excites the woman in me.

I scream inside. Nooo! Not him, please don't let it be him. As I roll over, I close my eyes and the only face staring back at me is his. Great just great, what on earth am I supposed to do now?

♥31

"Rachel, are you there?"

I hear Sally calling me and a quick glance at the clock by my bed tells me it's time to go. Quickly, I race downstairs without even checking my appearance and fling open the door. Sally looks at me strangely. "Um… are you ok, Rachel? I'm not interrupting anything am I?"

My hand flies to my face and I say in a strangely high voice, "No, I must have fallen asleep. Come in, I won't be long."

I race to the bathroom and the sight that greets me in the mirror makes my heart sink. My hair is wild and my eyes slightly crazed. Lipstick is smeared all over my mouth and the tears have left a trail down my cheeks. Splashing some cold water on my face, I set about repairing the damage.

Once I feel semi-presentable, I head back to meet Sally with a smile.

"Sorry, I must have fallen asleep in full makeup. I'm such an idiot."

She doesn't look convinced and yet smiles brightly.

"Well, this is it, Rachel. The day we've worked so hard to reach. How do you feel?"

I smile brightly. "To be honest, I'm all over the place. I suppose I've thought about it for so long and put so much effort into it, it doesn't seem real somehow. A bit like Christmas day. So much work goes into it and it's over in a flash."

She nods. "Never mind. Let's just hope it's successful."

As we walk to the village hall, I think about Max. "Have you seen Max since he got back?"

Sally is strangely evasive and shrugs, "No."

I blabber on. "That's a surprise. I suppose he's got his hands full with his guests."

She shrugs. "I suppose so."

I can tell she feels uncomfortable on the subject, so switch to one close to her heart. "Did you sell the paintings?"

She nods sadly. "Unfortunately, yes. They both sold, and I posted them out last week."

She doesn't sound happy about it and I feel bad. "Were they very special to you?"

She shrugs. "They were but I can paint another one."

I keep on pressing and say "Why were they so special?"

She shakes her head and sighs. "It wasn't so much the actual paintings. It was what inspired me to paint them. It was a happy time and I look back at it fondly. Max had just bought Bayside Manor, and we were helping him get it straight. I think it was then that I fell in love with the place. Everything was perfect in a way it never had been before. You see, I never had a friend as good as Max before. Jack and Max, well, they are the best friends a girl can have but Max and I were a little closer. That summer was perfect, Rachel. Finally, I had found a person who liked me for who I was and didn't judge me. Max loves my quirky ways and I never have to hide from him. I can be myself and that means more to me than anything. Those paintings reflected my happiness, and that's a little part of my past I wanted to keep."

I shake my head. "Then why sell them?"

She shrugs gloomily. "It seemed like a good idea at the time but now they've gone it's reinforced how much they meant to me. I'll always have the memories but those paintings, well, they were painted with love."

We see the village hall in front of us and notice quite a crowd gathering already.

Sally smiles weakly. "It looks as if it's quite a turnout, are you ready for this, Rachel?"

Taking her hand, I squeeze it hard and say with determination. "Readier than I'll ever be."

We share a smile and head towards the hall that so much rests on.

♥32

The hall looks magnificent as we head inside. Huge banners hang from the ceiling with 'Sally's Cake Sale,' emblazoned on a pink background. Bunting and pink balloons bring the hall to life and little tables are set out with white tablecloths and pretty daisies in jam jars. There are also banners calling to save Perivale and various leaflets litter every surface. At one end is a small stage set up with chairs where the Red Arrows are noisily teasing each other. They have their own banners and are dressed in their full regalia. I do a double take as I see them as a group. They are certainly impressive and I can only imagine how swamped they will be.

There are cakes set up alongside tea urns and donation pots for any loose change to help the fund. The hall looks amazing and the tears fill my eyes as I see the huge effort that everyone's made.

The local dignitaries are huddled in the corner and I see Bert and Sheila dishing out the teas and cakes to anyone who asks, in return for a donation. Then the doors open to the public and the place soon fills to capacity and we spill out onto the grass outside. The air is filled with laughter and loud conversation and the noise is deafening.

I watch Sally chatting to one of Max's friends and laugh as I see the protective arm he has around her shoulder. She looks amazing in a white dress with daisies on and her hair is white with pink streaks. Press photographers capture every minute of what is turning out to be an unqualified success.

Suddenly, a familiar hand finds mine and squeezes it hard and Jack says softly, "Well done, Rachel. You've worked so hard and it looks as if it's a huge success."

Turning to face him, I see the gentle, caring, man I love and try hard to bring my heart to its senses. I say softly, "It's down to all of us, Jack. We made this happen as a team."

Jack smiles and I watch as he looks past me and an expression I know a lot about flashes in his eyes. Turning in the direction of his gaze, I'm not surprised to see Fiona standing laughing with one of Max's friends. Jack watches them and I see it in his eyes. He hasn't got over her yet and probably never will.

As I look across, I picture them as a couple. They look right together and the hand I'm holding should never have let go of hers, so I say softly, "It's ok, Jack. Go to Fiona, she needs you and you need to be with her. It's pretty obvious."

He looks startled and shakes his head. "No, Rachel, you've got it wrong."

Smiling, I place my finger to his lips and say with feeling, "I haven't. You may want to forget her but your body betrays you. Don't turn your back on your future happiness because of your pride. We all do stupid things and can't help that. Just learn from it and move on."

I watch as Fiona's eyes flick in our direction and the look she gives him tells me everything I need to know. Giving him a gentle push, I say lightly, "It's fine. Go to her, Jack. Just be happy."

He shakes his head in confusion and says with concern. "What about you? I can't just leave you, for her."

Reaching up, I kiss him gently and whisper, "You were never mine to keep."

I see the emotion in his eyes as he says, "Thank you. You're a wonderful woman, Rachel. There aren't many like you."

I laugh softly, "Thank goodness for that. I'm not sure if that's a good thing or not."

I watch him walk towards Fiona and my heart settles. Yes, that was the right thing to do. Jack and Fiona were meant to be together; I know that now, and this feels right.

I'm aware of two people walking towards me and look up and see my father and Spencer looking completely out of place in the village hall in their suits and ties. Laughing, I head over to them and hug them warmly.

"Hey, I'm glad you made it."

My father smiles proudly. "You've done it again, sweetheart. Tell her your news, Spencer."

Spencer smiles and says excitedly, "We have the supermarket contract. The samples I sent over blew them away and they've ordered a point of sale for all their stores. Not just one supermarket either. The top four no less, so congratulations Rachel, you've done it again. Sally's cakes are set to be every bit as successful as the vegan ready meal range."

We all grin at each other with the elation only closing a big deal can bring. I hug them both and say emotionally, "Thank you so much, both of you. You've made this happen; I can't believe it."

My father laughs. "No, darling, you made this happen. We just did what we always do. Now, where is this wonder girl? I would love to meet her."

Laughing, I point her out still surrounded by Red Arrows and say proudly, "There she is, pretty in white."

Spencer looks surprised and I laugh softly. "Impressive, isn't she?"

He grins. "She's certainly different to what I imagined. Let's go and meet her."

We fight our way over to Sally and I introduce her to my father and Spencer. She looks at them with wide eyes and says shyly, "I'm pleased to meet you."

I leave them talking and look around the room for one person I'm aching to see. It takes me a while and then I see him standing with a group of people who must be his sponsors. My father appears beside me and follows my gaze, saying with interest. "Who are they?"

I smile and say in almost a whisper, "Logan Rivers. The man responsible for donating £50,000 to this project."

My father looks surprised. "I've heard that name before."

I nod. "Yes, he's some computer games whizz, you probably recognise it from that."

He shakes his head in confusion. "Hardly. You know me, I'm not one for computer games. No, I've heard it recently."

Spencer catches the tail end of the conversation and says, "Who are you talking about?"

My father says, "Does the name Logan Rivers ring any bells with you?"

Spencer nods. "Yes, it's the guy who owns Princeton holdings. The property company who bought Bluebell cottage."

My world stops spinning and everything turns black. The voices retreat into a weird, slow, void and I can only hear my mind racing out of control.

Logan owns Bluebell cottage. Not only that, he owns Honeysuckle cottage and never said a thing. He allowed us to worry all these months thinking they would be sold and yet he was the one who had the control.

His words spin around my mind as I hear him saying he would bulldoze it to the ground and rebuild a better one. I can hear him now, "The real value in this house is that view."

I can't even cry because the anger threatens to explode like a volcano. My father looks concerned. "Are you ok, Rachel?"

Spencer takes my arm and says, "Honey, are you ok?"

I just nod as a loud voice is heard calling everyone to listen.

"May I have your attention, please? My name is Bob Arnold and I'm the leader of the local council. We are all here for a very worthy cause that's close to everyone's hearts. This village hall in which you are standing has been at the heart of Perivale for several years and provided a much-loved centre for the community. Today, we are pleased to announce that the local council has received some very generous private funding to restore her for the good of future generations."

There are loud claps and cheers but they sound so far away to me as my brain struggles to accept what I've discovered.

He carries on. "I would like to thank Bintonu Industries for donating £50,000 by way of a charitable donation in honour of their newest computer game, designed by our local hero, Logan Rivers."

Everybody cheers and as I watch him nod, his eyes meet mine across the room. The daggers I throw him appear to take him by surprise and I see him tense as he stares at me with concern. I carry on staring as Bob carries on.

"I would also like to introduce Rachel Asquith, a new local resident who also happens to be the owner of Viking foods who have sponsored this event. You will all have sampled the delicious cakes of their new brand, Sally's cakes. Sally herself is also a much-loved local resident who was born and raised in Pembury and now lives in Perivale. She is more known for her Art but that will soon change as Sally's cakes are set to take the country by storm. Let's hear it for Sally and Rachel and Viking foods."

The noise is deafening and as I catch Sally's eyes, I feel bad. She looks absolutely mortified and I watch her shrink back in fear at the attention. My heart lifts as I see Max place his arm around her shoulder and squeeze it gently.

Then Bob says, "I also happen to know that two of Sally's paintings were sold bringing in a further £10,000 for the good cause. So, what with the sales generated by the cakes, the donation from Bintonu and the amount raised by the Red Arrows who we are honoured are here to support us, we can proudly announce that work on rebuilding Perivale village hall will start as soon as possible."

The noise is deafening and the cameras capture every bit of excitement. Looking around, I feel my heart settle. Whatever happens in the future, whether the hotel is built or the golf course goes ahead, one thing will always remain. What people can do when they put their heart and soul into it. What seemed like a pipe dream turned into a reality with some quick thinking and invaluable connections.

As the noise subsides my attention is caught by a familiar voice ringing out loud and clear. "May I have silence please?"

I look in surprise as Max jumps onto the stage and grabs the microphone from Bob. He looks into the crowd and I watch his eyes find Sally and the look he gives her takes my breath away.

He says loudly, "I just wanted to pay tribute to one person we have already met. Sally Mumble, the pretty vision in white, who has talent running through her blood."

Sally looks horrified and Max laughs. "Sally, you like to hide away in your little cottage because you think the world can't see what we all see clearer than a cloudless sky. There is nobody as special as you and I have something I need to say."

Sally looks confused as Max jumps down and fights his way through the crowd. "Sally, we've been friends for many years and nobody means more to me than you. You wonder what brings me back and I'm looking at her. You have given so much to the community on this project and I want to give something back to you."

He gestures to one of his team who hands him a package wrapped in brown paper. Max offers it to Sally and says gently, "It's for you, babe. A present from me to you."

With shaking fingers, Sally unwraps the package and I see her eyes fill with tears as she says with emotion, "My paintings."

The tears fall as she gasps, "You bought me my own paintings."

The crowd laughs and Max grins. "I couldn't let them go, babe. I know how much they mean to you and wanted you to always have them. Which brings me to the real reason I grabbed this mic. Sally, you think of me as a friend but I want to be more than that. I love you not just as a friend but as the woman I want to spend the rest of my life with. I can't imagine a future without you in it and I want to grow old with you. You are the beat of my heart and the breath in my body. I can't function without you and you bring a happy kind of crazy to my life. What do you say, babe, will you be my girl forever?"

I think the whole hall holds its breath as they look at Sally. The expression on her face says it all and is looking at Max as if he's the only one in the room. The connection they share is palpable and the light shines from her eyes as she says softly, "I always have been and always will be."

The crowd parts as Max crosses the room towards her and takes her in his arms. My tears join the rest of the women's in the room as he lowers his lips to hers and they share their first kiss.

The noise in the room is deafening as everyone shouts their congratulations and I add my voice to theirs with a happiness that makes me believe in happy ever afters.

My father says with amazement, "Well I'll be damned. That was some speech he just made. You know, I think I may just move here myself if this is what this place is made of."

I nod in agreement. "Yes, this place is special alright. I just hope it stays that way."

♥33

Later that evening, when the dust has settled and life has returned to the sleepy village one we all crave, I allow myself to think of Logan. I managed to avoid him for the rest of the day because I couldn't trust myself to speak to him. I had to push everything aside and concentrate on why we were there and did what I've always done - become the professional machine that gets me results.

However, now I'm alone in my little piece of paradise, I allow all the hurt and betrayal to wash over me, ridding me of any feelings I thought I had for the man who brings out the beast in me. Sadly, however there is one feeling I just can't shake - I want him. I want him so badly it hurts. Why can't I cut him out of my life after what he's done?

A steady tap on the door brings me back to the present and I sigh. Visitors at this late hour. I'd hoped to hang that smile I had pasted on my face on the shelf along with all my hopes and dreams for the night. However, this has not been an ordinary day and I expect its Sally come to fill me in on what happened.

No such luck as I open the door revealing the one person my head never wants to see again but my traitorous heart can't let go of. Logan.

The look I throw him must say it all because he grabs my hand and pulls me into my own cottage. Spinning me around he says sternly, "Speak."

He frowns as my eyes flash angrily. "What right have you to barge in here and demand answers?"

I laugh bitterly, "Oh yes, I forgot, you have every right because apparently, you're the proud new owner of Bluebell cottage."

I watch as the realisation dawns and he shrugs. "So, why is that a problem?"

Snatching my hand away, I move across the room to get as much distance as I can between us. "What's the problem?"

I almost scream. "I'll tell you the problem, you knew how worried I was, sorry *we* were, about the fate of this place. You could have told us not to worry, and this was one problem that was resolved. But you didn't, and that makes me wonder why? Is it because you saw a golden opportunity to make more money and had two of the properties needed to make a killing? Or was it because you wanted this for yourself and intend on bulldozing the place to the ground to make way for some modern monstrosity of your own? Whatever your reason, it's a selfish one and that, my angry friend, is the reason every ounce of respect I ever had for you was left in that village hall today. You're a selfish man, Logan Rivers and you deserve the lonely life you crave."

I have to turn away because my harsh words even wound my soul. I can't help it, I'm so angry, disappointed and feel a loss of something I never knew I had until today.

I feel a hand on my shoulder and shrug it off angrily. However, that hand won't allow it and Logan spins me around and holds me tightly against him. I can't move as he whispers, "How could I tell you? If I told you I was the new owner, it would change everything."

I pull back in surprise and see the storm raging in his eyes. I almost gasp as I see the emotion directed at me and my knees feel weak as the confusion sets in. I whisper, "What do you mean?"

He sighs heavily and draws me over to the window where the moon lights up the bay, casting a magical light over the unusually still sea. "This view, this cottage, this place, is your fairy tale, Rachel. You told me you wanted the fairy tale and yet I could see you making the same mistake over and over again. I approached Molly long before we learned of Christopher Masters plan for this place. I went to see her the day after we met. The morning before I went to London, I paid her a visit and asked her to give me first refusal when she sold. I bought this cottage to keep your dream alive. You see, I knew from the minute I hauled you into the boat that you were the woman for me. You were magnificent that day, Rachel. Strong, brave and courageous with a vulnerability that brought out the protective side in me."

He strokes my hair and holds me close as he says emotionally, "Then you met Jack and thought he was the one you were searching for. I watched you falling in love with him and even then, I knew he was wrong for you. Men like Jack don't belong with women like you, Rachel. He is nice, dependable and normal but you need more. I know that because I'm the same. We are always looking for the opportunity. We don't see problems only challenges and we see life differently to most. We appreciate the beauty of nature and have a strong urge to improve on a masterpiece. You would have been bored with Jack as soon as you realised there was something missing in your life. You see, we may escape from the world but we crave the excitement it brings just as much as the solitude we desire."

He pulls back and his eyes sparkle with lust and he growls, "You need a man who loves you unconditionally. Someone who will always put you first, even if it means trouble for them. Somebody who thinks you're the sun in the sky and the moon at night. A man who craves your touch more than anything and can't think straight when you're around. I am that man, Rachel because the last few months have been the most painful of my life yet the most intense. I have fallen in love with the perfect woman bar one thing."

I look at him anxiously. "Which is?"

He rolls his eyes, "She just won't remove those bloody rose-coloured spectacles and see the obvious staring at her in the face. She looks for the right things in the wrong person and doesn't believe that magic can be dressed up in its darkest form."

My eyes flash angrily, "And you are that magic I suppose?"

He nods cockily. "You know I am. You're just fooling yourself if you think I'm not. You ask me why I never told you about Bluebell cottage? How could I when it would reveal the one thing I wanted you to discover naturally?"

He smiles softly, "That I love you with all my heart and always will. I bought Bluebell cottage for you, Rachel. To protect your fairy tale and your future happiness. You may never have known it was me but I wanted to give you something you would always cherish. Your future."

His words wrap around my heart like a much-loved friend. Any doubts I ever had are kept firmly out of the cosy bubble he has created. As he spoke, every word he said pulled in all the puzzle pieces that had been spinning around me desperate to complete the picture. As I look into his eyes, I smile softly, "Then you know what happens next, Logan."

He looks confused. "What's that?"

I smile happily. "In all good fairy tales, they share love's true kiss and live happily ever after."

He smiles wickedly. "I'm no prince, Rachel. If you saw where my mind was right now it would shatter that cosy little fairy tale into a million pieces. However, I'm happy to oblige with the kiss and the happy ever after. Just make sure you do as I say and we'll be fine."

Grinning, I push him away and roll my eyes. "You are seriously going to argue with my happy ever after moment. I can't believe you would do that. I've waited for my prince to come charging in and rescue me from my own stupidity and I get you. Maybe I should sleep for 100 years and when I wake up, you will have learned how this thing is supposed to work. For goodness sake, Logan don't you know anything?"

He pulls me against him hard and dips me to the ground gallantly. Leaning down, he growls. "Maybe this fairy tale is more Beauty and Beast. Now I'm going to show you that beast in me."

I laugh softly, "Stop talking, Logan. You just don't know when to stop."

Then there are no more words. No more recriminations and no more explanations needed. It's all in the kiss we share. Explosive, sexy and the stuff of legends. It's true, happy ever afters do exist, you just have to tiptoe through the broken dreams and misunderstandings to find them.

♥Epilogue
One Year Later

"You know, I'll never get tired of this view."

Logan squeezes my shoulder gently as we sit on the beach looking out across the bay. Much like I did just over a year ago but now I have someone to share it with. The man I came here not knowing I'd find. The man who was always my destiny and yet was hiding away in a little piece of paradise.

The sunlight catches the diamond on my finger and bounces off a nearby rock. I hold up my finger and admire the polished perfection that reminds me every day how lucky I am.

Logan reaches out and laces my fingers with his. "Are you happy, Rachel?"

Snuggling into him, I say happily, "Why are you asking me a dumb question like that? Of course, I am. Who wouldn't be when she's living the dream?"

Laughing, he pushes me down on to the sand and rolls on top of me pinning my arms by my side. "Just checking because I know how foolish you can be. Knowing you, you'd wake up one day and question whether rain is real. You're a difficult woman."

Pretending to frown, I say quickly, "Says you. The man who stomps around angrily most of the time and sulks if he can't spend the day playing with his toys outside."

He rolls over and pulls me on top of him and brings my face to his and whispers, "You're my favourite toy, I'd play with you all day if I could."

Our lips meet as we hear, "For god's sake you two, don't you ever stop?"

Sitting up, we both grin as we see Sally and Max watching us standing hand in hand. Laughing, they sit down heavily beside us and Max draws Sally between his knees and puts his arms around her hugging her to him as he always does. Max says cheerily, "So, what's the plan then?"

I smile happily. "We're meeting up with Jack and Fiona and Bert and Sheila at the beach house. We have some planning to do and need everyone's input."

Sally smiles. "It will be just like old times."

Max laughs. "We're quite the formidable team. We should have a name, what about The Perivale Rangers or The Perivale Plotters?"

Sally giggles. "Rubbish, you need to think of something better than that."

She snuggles into him and sighs. "You know, I still can't believe that golf course is going ahead. I never thought it would somehow and I'm not sure how I feel about it."

I nod. "I'm the same. Part of me thinks if anything was going to be built here, that's the best solution. At least it preserves the wide-open spaces and means people can enjoy the place."

Logan nods. "Well, it's far enough away not to bother us. At least this is a little corner of the world that will never change."

I laugh in disbelief. "Says the man who is currently bringing those cottages kicking and screaming into the modern world."

Sally laughs. "Yes, but the plans just enhance not change. They will look amazing when you've finished, Logan."

He stretches out looking pleased with himself. "Yes, I'm quite proud of them. From the outside they look as they would have done all those years ago when they were first built. A fresh coat of paint and a pretty landscaped garden just makes them even prettier. However, inside they will contain all the latest modern conveniences sitting side by side the traditional. Wooden floors and wood burners will re-create the past, yet the modern appliances and bi-fold doors will make living there easier and allow the outside in. Yes, I think it was a good compromise."

Sally looks at us with interest. "Will you move there when it's finished?"

Logan and I share a look and I smile ruefully. This was a constant battle that has finally been resolved. At first, I wanted to live there with no alterations. Logan wanted us to live in the beach house and rent out Bluebell cottage.

I look at Sally and shake my head. "No, we've decided to rent it out along with Honeysuckle cottage. It just made more sense for us to live in the beach house. Bluebell cottage is smaller and we would soon outgrow it. Besides, I wanted to let the magic of the place change another person's life. I'm hoping somebody moves in who will appreciate the magic of the place as much as I did."

Logan rubs my shoulder and kisses the top of my head lightly. I snuggle into him as I always do and feel content and happy.

Max grins. "When do Jack and Fiona get the keys to Honeysuckle cottage? We should make them throw a housewarming party."

Logan smiles. "Work should finish in a couple of months, just in time for the summer." He looks at his watch. "We had better get moving, they'll be here soon."

We jump up and dust the sand from our clothes and walk together along the beach. Logan and Max hang back a little and their laughter floats towards us as I slip my arm in Sally's and we chat happily. She laughs. "What a difference a year makes. Look at us now. You and Logan are about to become parents and Max and I are planning a wedding. Jack and Fiona are starting their married life in my old home and Bert and Sheila are, '*The* Facebook' ninjas."

Bert and Sheila became completely obsessed by Facebook. They have so many friends on there I can't count them and have joined several groups and reconnected with old acquaintances. It's certainly made a difference to their lives and I laugh as I see then embracing technology as if they're teenagers again.

As the sun shines down on us, it reminds me how lucky I am. I really do have it all. I still run Viking foods but do it from the beach house three days a week and spend two in London. Logan always comes with me and we stay in an apartment close to the River Thames.

Spencer bought the apartment we used to share and is happy playing the field and enjoying life as a single man. Sally is a rich woman and not just because Sally's cakes was an overnight success and have now gone international. No, she is richer because of the love she found with Max. They live in Bayside Manor when they're not travelling with the Red Arrows. That's all about to change though as Max's stint in the display team is coming to an end. They are about to be married which is what we will be planning later.

The guys catch up and I feel Logan's hand slip into mine. As Max picks Sally up and runs with her towards the sea, kicking and screaming, Logan says softly, "I love you, Rachel, you've made me the happiest man in the world."

Squeezing his hand, I say, "You know, Logan, if it's a girl, can we call her Cinderella?"

He rolls his eyes. "Maybe I should amend that statement. Rachel, you've made me the most irritated man in the world."

Shrugging, I pat my stomach and say happily, "Just kidding, I always preferred Belle. After all, as fairy tales go that one's the closest to my heart."

Logan laughs and spins me around and pulls me close and says sweetly, "You'll always be my happy ever after."

Then he kisses me as deeply as he always does. Intense, demanding and so sexy it makes my head spin. Just like the man himself, the one I never thought I'd find and almost passed him by when I did.

Thank goodness for the magic of fairy tales and Bluebell cottage.

The End

♥

Thank you for reading Fooling in Love.

If you liked it, I would love if you could leave me a review, as I must do all my own advertising.

This is the best way to encourage new readers and I appreciate every review I can get. Please also recommend it to your friends, as word of mouth is the best form of advertising. It won't take longer than two minutes of your time, as you only need write one sentence if you want to.

Have you checked out my website? Subscribe to keep updated with any offers or new releases.

sjcrabb.com

sjcrabb.com

More books by S J Crabb

The Diary of Madison Brown
My Perfect Life at Cornish Cottage
My Christmas Boyfriend
Jetsetters
More from Life
A Special Kind of Advent
Fooling in love
Will You

sjcrabb.com